LAKE OF SIN

Prince of Lust #4

LUCIEN BURR

LAKE OF SIN
Lucien Burr

Edited by Drew McBlain

Cover Art by 4RESNA

Book Design by Lucien Burr

Ebook design by Lucien Burr

This book is a work of fiction and as such all characters and situations are fictitious. Any resemblance to actual people, places or events is coincidental.

Category (Adult Erotic Fiction)
Genre (Paranormal/ Romance / LGBT)

CONTENT WARNINGS

Occult, submission and dominance, physical abuse, moral degradation, religious themes, religious mockery, extreme sexual activity

Please note:

All sigils are in the public domain.

Original source: THE BOOK OF THE GOETIA OF SOLOMON THE KING (1904), S.L. MacGregor Mathers and Aleister Crowley

PROLOGUE

Now the works of the flesh are evident: sexual immorality, impurity, sensuality, idolatry, sorcery, enmity, strife, jealousy, fits of anger, rivalries, dissensions, divisions, envy, drunkenness, orgies, and things like these. I warn you, as I warned you before, that those who do such things will not inherit the kingdom of God.

Galatians 5:19-21

PLEASURE IS A SIN.

Some will debate this. Some will flounder through the Bible for glimpses of God dallying in joyous things. My brethren would say the world we occupy is fallen, that perversions are inevitable, and that pleasure as God knows it is impossible to have here. But I say: *Our* pleasures are unobtainable for God Himself. I say: Pleasure is a sin, for God is jealous. God is *jealous*! God doesn't want other things in life to usurp His place; He is as covetous and paranoid as a jilted lover; He falls into the sin of His own designs.

He had a body in Christ. He would have tasted the pleasures of satisfying hunger, of thirst, of the pulsing pull of arousal. I ask: Is that why His Son had to die? Is that why He removed Himself from the face of the earth, if just to free Himself from the burden of desire?

The Bible says: *Delight yourself in the* LORD, *and he will give you the desires of your heart.* Psalm 37:4

What bullshit. I wasted my life waiting for Him to absolve me of desire. After my time with Furfur, I knew a sweetness could be achieved in pleasure. I realised that in seeking pleasure, I had been seeking punishment, too. Not the kind I revelled in, but the kind that would truly hurt. I sought the pain not for absolution, but for confirmation of this truth:

Not only were the bishops and my fellow priests right to question me, but my disgrace was inevitable. I threw the words *destiny* and *fate* around and hoped they were as real as the Devil himself.

But what if I had *chosen* this? What if I had taken back my life and chosen to give it to hedonism, and pleasure, and joy, and to forsake everything else?

What would that mean, then?

Could that mean I might approach Asmodeus and my ascent to its throne not out of duty, but out of desire? Out of want?

Would that not make me even more worthy to sit by its side?

❧ I ❧

I sat in the wake of Furfur's departure with revelations dripping over my flesh.

I had been given pleasure, and I had taken pleasure. These were new developments for me, new waters to wade through, but I was thrilled. To have more ways to use my body made me a better servant. In a selfish way, it would excite me further. The prospect of being used sounded ever more delicious with the thought that I could experience pleasure too. . .

Why hadn't I dreamt of that before? So used to being God's servant, I had never considered having another serve me. I thought of Galatians 1: *"For am I now seeking the approval of man, or of God? Or am I trying to please man? If I were still trying to please man, I would not be a servant of Christ."*

I wondered: *Am I seeking the approval of God, or the devil? Am I seeking the approval of myself?*

I was no servant of Christ, no bitch to be lead. With the Earl of Asmodeus' Circle satisfied, I had three more to meet before my Lord permitted me to stand before it. I needed to experience pleasure with a Marquis, a Prince, and a Duke of Hell.

I should have stayed silent and dutiful, committing myself to the final three before

I kept Asmodeus in my heart, and I called out to it.

"Do you hear me?"

It answered immediately, "I hear you."

The wind carried the booming voice of Asmodeus. Beneath me, jet-black waves tossed themselves against the rocks with raucous cracks. I breathed in deep, sulphur settling into my lungs, and found I did not know what to say. I had Asmodeus' attention and no thoughts to share.

I wanted my Lord to calm me, and I wanted to hear it was proud of me. I wanted it to tell me I was worthless beyond my body, and yet I also craved to feel important. I wanted it to know I did this out of a kind of love and as a bid for my future. I sought eternal pleasure, yes, but also a chance to be eternally myself. To embrace every vicious want in me.

Eventually, I said, "Three left to pleasure, my Lord."

Asmodeus' hum of approval rumbled over the earth, shaking the land.

And then, without thinking, I said, "Will *you* please *me*, when I am by your side?"

I had never been so bold to Asmodeus before. Shivering, I remembered the strength of its appearance when it had come to me in the monastery. It had thrown me across the room; it had possessed the power to crush me, and without a doubt, it could do the same to me if it wished. Most likely, it could have done a lot worse since I had existed fully in its realm.

The sky darkened, and the rumbling turned unhappy. Still, I did not throw myself into apology. I stayed seated, fingers pressed against the warm, rough stone of Furfur's circle, and I waited for punishment, or for words.

And the world changed.

Shadow fell over the land. More than shadow—a darkness so dense I could see nothing. Then, flashing out from the fog, a clawed red hand shot toward me.

I couldn't move. Fingers clutched around my neck and hauled me up. Instantly, all the pressure clogged in my throat, and with my trachea crushed, no air could get in. I thrashed. I kicked weakly at nothing, and no face resolved from the shadows, no more of the body. I knew Asmodeus was enraged with me. It ruled this plane, and I had overstepped.

"You little cretin. You whore. You, who I plucked from inconsequence to lead to bodily glory!"

Its voice boomed thunderous. Sound crowded into my ears, a stench of sulphur into my nostrils. What little air I could get down, I gagged on.

"You defy me now? So close to the end, to your prize? You have already given me your soul; if your body is not mine, then you are worthless!"

But that wasn't what I had meant at all. I struggled to speak. All that came out was, "To be... *better*!"

An outraged scoff. A chime sounded somewhere, and discordant trumpets, and I remembered Asmodeus had been an angel, once: a grand design from God's hand. "Better? Better!"

It released me, and I dropped. No ground rushed up to meet me. I fell and fell for a small eternity, and when I accepted the fall—the constant flip of my stomach, the rise of fear in my body—and recovered from the choking, I spoke again.

"A true servant of the flesh should know his own wants!"

Suddenly the ground was there. I landed and rolled, my poor body flinching from expected pain. The fog of darkness still enveloped me, but Asmodeus had not spoken again. So, I went onto my knees and tried again, this time with proper decorum.

"I propose that I am not fully a whore until I can beg for everything I want. I say that one of the demons I pleasured —" and I paused, reframing, "—that I experienced pleasure *with*, showed me this. I am still a creature of shame. I wish not to be, before I come to you, my Lord."

For a long time, there was no response. I braced myself for the possibility that this was my punishment. I was set to languish in the umbral dark for as long as Asmodeus wished. But then two red eyes blinked open in the dark, and Asmodeus was there with me.

"Lord." I pushed myself fully into the ground. My heart raced, like my body could tell this was the *real* form of Asmodeus, not the watery shade I had managed to summon back in the abbey. "Your demons will tell you how loyal I am to you. I dedicate my life and my eternity to you. But I cannot fully be your creature if I do not know myself."

The haze dissipated slowly, impenetrable black becoming a soft twilight. When it next spoke, Asmodeus' voice had taken on a new, softer tone.

"You continue to surprise me, little blasphemer."

I did not know if this was a compliment or a critique, and so I stayed unmoving in my bow.

"You *now* are so very different to the man who summoned me."

Something sharp pressed beneath my soft palate and I was forced to raise my head. A sharp nail bed against my flesh; I gulped as I looked into the porous red eyes of Asmodeus and found them full of interest. There was nothing else to see beyond its eyes, but they seduced me.

The fingers moved to clench my cheeks, nails digging hard against the soft flesh. *Pop me*, I thought. *Leave a mark. Make me yours.*

"Do what you must to free yourself from the shackles of your shame. Delight in pleasure. And if you lure my demons into touching you how you wish to be touched, then you are even more alluring than I first expected."

It felt. . .*good* to hear that. I shivered with relief and glanced up. Though Asmodeus had not fully appeared before me, those red eyes stared at me.

And the devil winked.

✵ 2 ✵

When Asmodeus left with a little more than a heavy, lust-filled sigh, the darkness surrounding me lifted fully.

I was no longer sequestered on Furfur's tiny island of stone and sea. The smoke of Asmodeus' rage cleared, and I had been left on a hilltop overlooking a great stone structure.

It was circular and large, its walls high and the stone was a brushed white. Turrets sprouted from it at various intervals, and dozens of flags and ripped fabric waved in the wind.

The place looked awfully like something from Earth. The longer I looked, the more the structure resolved into the familiar, into something I could recognise.

A fort.

I walked carefully down the hillside to approach the structure, which was the only thing of note for miles and miles. A grey desert seeped into the distance, spreading from the back of the stone fort and creeping to the very edge of the horizon. But to the front of the fort and beneath this brown grassy hill was ground that would kill me. Lava split between black rock, oozing free, flames spitting and dancing above it. A single survivable path was raised above the licks of lava, made of onyx-black stone. Weapons of unburning steel framed it, a line of jagged, interlocking spears, swords, and great sledgehammers providing cover for travellers approaching the fort.

I wasted no time. My conversation with Asmodeus had invigorated me. With all the hubris only a mortal man can bear, I scrambled naked down the hill and walked over the hot glass-like rock. Flames leapt in the air on either side of me. My skin blistered and healed every second, the soles of my feet grew charcoal black. Still, I walked. The pain never hit its crescendo, not when the promise of pleasure drove me forward.

Everywhere was the sound of the lava's hiss and of—fighting. Beyond the titan walls of the fort, I heard the clang of armour and swords, and I thought of knights. Trumpets and a discordant singing roared around me.

At the end of that long path, a small plaque sat flush beside the deep-set doors. It glistened in gold and declared:

DESIGNED BY MULCIBER

Which meant nothing to me at all.

With my jaw clenched and my human fear held at bay by willpower alone, I pressed against the great door. It loomed above me, taller than a tower, and my pressing barely did anything. Nothing budged. So, petulant like a child, I called out, "I am here for the Marquis!"

What did I expect? Nothing happened. I was one human voice struggling against a cacophony of hellish discord. Nothing could be done, but neither could I wait there. I tried the door again for good measure, and every underworked muscle in my flesh pulsed and ached.

I cast about. The walls were too sheer and too tall for me to climb. The lava spat and pulsed. Would my body burn if I leapt into it? Would the skin slough off? Would the burns ever heal? I wondered if Asmodeus would appreciate such a display of despair at my own inability to reach the Marquis, or if I would be made so hideous my Lord would abandon me forever.

I had been staring into the lava for so long that I barely registered how close I'd moved to the edge. The nearness let the heat scathe my skin, and I blinked rapidly, inhaling sulphur and heat and the scent of my own sweat.

But the nearness allowed me to better see the edge of the fort. A tiny width of stone jutted from its base and encircled the entire fort. If I could balance and stay close to the wall, it would make a near-insubstantial way forward, a path only a fool would follow.

Of course, I was on it within moments.

I pressed my body flush to the stone, which scraped gently against my skin. Flame and heat licked at my back and sweat pricked at the arch that housed my tailbone. Those discordant trumpets continued blaring; none knew I was skirting around like vermin trying to find a way in.

I shuffled around the warm stone, and not once did I question what I was doing or what I had become. I wasn't any less filled with lust than I had been. The touch of stone against my body wasn't sobering; I felt perfectly sane as I moved. It took minutes, nearly a half hour, to get halfway around the bend. The sea of lava stopped abruptly where it met the grey sand, but I was in no mood to test whether said sand was any less dangerous, recalling the sea of grass around Furcus' library and the poison it held. I remained pressed to the wall and found, eventually, a door.

Which was naturally a surprising thing to find halfway around a hellish fort after passing a sea of lava.

The door itself was very plain. It wouldn't have looked out of place in the monastery. A simple, dark wood with a wooden doorknob. I reached out and turned it, and nearly fell backwards when I realised it was unlocked.

Thankfully, it swung inwards. It scraped over stone, and its hinges shrieked. I went rigid on instinct, straining to hear if the music or the distant clamour had stopped for me. Nothing. I peered into the fort and found I had been deposited in something like a hellish armoury.

Cautiously, I stepped inside. The door slammed shut behind me without intervention, and I spooked, stumbling back against something thin and metal. It fell, clanging onto the stone, disturbing several other things: a giant scoop of steel that could have been a shield for a giant, a spearhead laid next to it and utterly unattached to a pole, and some unnameable objects I had no reference for that were sharp, triangular prisms inlaid with jewels. The space was dark and cluttered. Metal rods crisscrossed overhead, and as I got my bearings, I understood that they were weapons: weapons triple the size of my body, laid haphazardly in a dusty corner. Indeed, this entire room appeared abandoned.

Light spilled in through a door to the right. Though the first door I'd encountered had been human-sized, this archway loomed large. I shivered at the thought of the body that might fit through that door.

I shivered, though not entirely with fear.

I wasted no time snooping in the armoury and instead made for that door. At the edge of the threshold, I peered around the corner and saw what was happening.

A battle. Some kind of fray.

On flat ground, arena-like and dusty, two giants engaged in battle. The hilts of their weapons were interlocked, and they hissed and growled at each other. There were demons or must have been: one had purple skin rippling with boils, wings and claws sprouting from its flesh. The other had eerily pale skin and the head of a lion. Sweat permeated the air.

They roared and shoved back from one another. The lion-head thrust forward and skewered one of its opponent's eyes. Black blood oozed from the eye socket, and as it wrenched its arm backwards, the eye popped free. The purple demon howled with rage.

But there were too many banners, too much noise, too much music for it to be a *true* battle—and a crowd was watching, I realised. Impish voyeurs gathered in the shadows and chittered or floated above next to demonic cherubim. They were four that I could see, and all of the cherubim were a tetrad of earth creatures. They each had four faces: of a lion, an ox, an eagle, and a man, and pressed to the lips of the human face was a trumpet clutched by two human hands. But they had the hoofed feet of a cow and four blackened, stringy wings.

A tournament, then, or a festival.

I don't know what I was thinking. I crept out from the armoury like they would embrace me with open arms. Me! Nothing more than a naked, desperate human! I ran out with too much confidence, arms open to the Heavens, and I cried out, "I am here to meet the Marquis!"

The music stopped abruptly. The cherubim spun around and cast their four sets of eyes upon me, sixteen ghoulish faces bearing down on me from above. The imps on the ground began to whisper. Growls emerged from the giants. They slumped, their weapons drooping from their arms.

I lowered my arms.

Then, I was roughly yanked from the ground. I kicked the air. Pressure clutched at my waist, and I looked down helplessly to find fingers the size of my forearm wrapped around my midsection. All the air escaped my lungs in a rush.

I had been plucked up by a giant I hadn't seen, one posted flush to the wall I had just run around.

I tried to twist in its grip, craning to see who had me. It

had a strange, pig-like face. Great tusks curled from its cracked lips, and a myriad of eyes exploded over its forehead and half its skull. Long black tresses fell from the other half. It snorted, and I flinched back from the spray of saliva.

It seemed to be waiting. I didn't know what to do. Cautiously, I stretched my head back, trying to see the others in the frozen tableau I stumbled upon, but the world was upside down. I flung myself back up and asked, "Marquis?"

Its expression changed minutely. Its eyes narrowed. Such a human display, I almost forgot what was holding me. The beast leaned forward and inhaled so hard its nostrils flared wide, and then it scrunched its features up into horrified disgust. Very gently, it put me down.

We all stood there in silence. Then, the two giants whose tournament I'd interrupted paced away from the centre of the arena, but not before one kicked three times, dragging its foot over the ground.

I walked forward and saw that it had disturbed the dust, and beneath that lay the sigil.

AND I WENT to my knees before it.

All the demons watched me and said nothing. I had no weapon with which to open my veins, and so I raised my hands like I was begging for an offering. The two giants exchanged a long look. The lion-head moved first. It reached for the sword at its scabbard and removed it with a sharp *schling!* of a sound, and carefully pointed the tip of the blade towards my palm. I did not shiver nor shake, even when anticipatory nausea started up. The blade pressed like a fat pin into the palm of my hand, and wet runnels of blood welled up and seeped through the grooves in my palm. I cupped my proffered blood and brought it down to the sigil, and after I let the blood run into every nook and cranny, I cupped my bloody hand around my limp cock for good measure, to reconfirm my body as part of the rite.

A growl started up from the armoury. I looked up in time with dozens of heads to see black smog crawling from the shadowy room. The imps began to whisper and giggle and whine, and the cherubim blasted one final note on their trumpets, a sound that heralded new arrival and ended the festivities all at once. They fled quickly, the four of them peeling off with squeals and layered cries echoing from their four heads and shared throat. When they were gone, the giants stomped away, each of them flanking the sigil where I still knelt.

I returned to the shadow, craning to see.

A bloody, rough-pelted wolf sprinted from the centre of the darkness. Two great wings were folded against its back, the grey feathers lifting from the speed of its approach. A serpent tail whipped furiously in the air, and the panting of the wolf became the only sound. A metre from the sigil, the beast skidded to a halt. Thick saliva dripped from its yellowed teeth. It panted laboriously, and even from a distance, I could smell its rankness; a dense smell, like old fish and something septic. I gagged.

"Are you the Marquis of this kingdom of Hell?" I whispered.

The wolf opened its mouth, and something spewed forth: flame or light—something so bright I could hardly bear to stare at it. The sound, like rushing water or an all-consuming fire, persisted on and on without end. I forced myself to look, to really peer into the brightness. The light warbled, rippling with movement. And I heard the name whispered from the wolf's throat, edging out of its jaw, and then echoed in susurrus voices:

MARCHOSIAS.

I understood, and yet couldn't comprehend. Marquis Marchosias was not the wolf, but the thing spewing forth from its open mouth. Intangible flame, ungraspable light: I had no pleasure at the sight of it and couldn't think of what I might do to it.

With my nerves still bludgeoned, I said, "I am sent by Lord Asmodeus Itself. Stand before me as a man!"

Marchosias, or the wolf carrying its spirit, let out a strangled cry. The flame still burned, and I thought I could see two eyes gleaming at me from the rippling white light.

A voice like a deep scrape hissed, "YOU WISH TO SPEAK WITH ME?"

I pushed off the ground and bowed my head. "I do."

Then, "YOU ARE HUMAN."

I told it as I told many of the demons I had serviced: "I have relinquished all mortal rights. I have betrayed my honourable self for this life. Lord Asmodeus wishes me to prove myself to it. Come before me as a man so we may speak more properly."

I could not tell you where my fear went. Abruptly, the wolf shut its jaw, and a great hacking and writhing began in its body. When it next heaved, a wet, slick-covered ball of a figure emerged wetly from its mouth and landed in the dust, sending sand into the air. The saliva-coated limbs unfurled from its foetal position and rapidly grew into a man until it was the size of the other giants in the arena.

The wolf—deflated. As if all the nutrients in its body had evaporated, it became nothing more than an empty skin, a pelt collapsing onto the stone.

Marchosias had not heeded my exact request. Though its body resembled a human man, too much was inhuman. Its head remained wolfish. It appeared messy, the fur thick and knotted around the neck, and as if its head had bloomed suddenly from a wound rather than a creature born this way. I half expected to see puckering sutures around the neck, but no such thing existed. Its shoulders were broad, and its chest very hairy. At times, I was certain the human hair gave way to a pelt. Its feet were that of a wolf's, too, and those two grey wings were neatly overlapping at its back.

What frightened me most was its cock, which wasn't a cock at all, but the new source of Marchosias' infernal, intangible light.

I panted hard, backing away from Marchosias. The demon stomped forward out of the circle; there was no point in running. I could have sprinted, and it would have caught me in seconds. I looked up in time to watch its arm swing through the air, hand slamming into my waist. I gasped, let out a shuddery sob as it lifted me from the ground, and like the other giant before it, the Marquis held me aloft to inspect me.

"CONTINUE," it ordered loudly, clomping to the right. My head spun as I bounced through the air. With a wave of its fingers, a bright light appeared in the fort, and a new section materialised: a tremendous throne positioned three stairs in the air, at the height the cherubim had been lurking at. Sounds started up beneath us as it climbed, and by the time Marchosias was seated, the tournament had recommenced below us.

But I was hardly concerned by the battle between lesser demons. Marchosias lowered me onto its thigh. I straddled it, legs slipping either side of the warm trunk of a leg. To my right, the light from its nethers blinded me, and so I scooted back and craned up at the demon—who resolutely didn't look my way. It was completely transfixed by the events happening below.

I swallowed and asked, "Will you speak to me?"

"At some point."

"I need to pleasure you. Or you may pleasure me. But it is necessary to proceed."

"Is this some kind of punishment?"

"What?" I tried to stand on the demon's leg, my ego bruised. "Why would you say that?"

Marchosias hesitated. Despite its size, it did not frighten me, not the way Asmodeus did. When the Marquis finally spoke, it only gestured below and said, "This is what brings me pleasure."

I let it watch for a time before I began to question what this was about. A sadness loomed in this arena—or a kind of human pettiness. It was a feeling I had never associated with infernal beings, nor angelic beings, but with hopeless men. Ones whose ventures in farming had gone unrewarded, ones whose crops suffered in the gruelling heat, or whose children contracted some malaise.

How strange to be seated on the lap of an eternal creature, one of God's fallen angels, and think: a depression rots it.

And it had been an angel, hadn't it?

"Your wings," I prompted. Instantly, I felt the demon tense.

It did not look down at me, but it asked, "WHAT OF THEM?"

I didn't say anything more. I could hear the twist in its voice, the nudge towards anger. But where the cherubim had wings of leather, and other demons' showed signs of decay and disuse, Marchosias' wings were pristine.

"They're beautiful." It was truthful, but it also felt right to say. Or assume. Marchosias took pride in its wings, if not in any other part of its appearance. It seemed to me that the cleanliness of its feathers and the neatness of them were manufactured.

My comment prompted the demon to look down at me. It plucked me up by a single arm, raising me high, and my full body weight dangled from between the pinch of its forefinger and thumb. It raised me up to its eyes: wide, shrewd things.

"YOU SMELL OF HELL. YOU HAVE BEEN HERE LONG ENOUGH. WHAT MAKES YOU SO SPECIAL THAT I MUST CAST MY EYE UPON YOU? YOU ARE LIKE ANY OTHER HUMAN: TOO SURE THAT YOUR BELIEF IN GOD MADE YOU ABOVE MY KIND."

"I was a priest," I told it, and I explained the whole sorry business. I let it know the truth about what I think. That I had forsaken God, that I wish to let my desires rule me. That they *had* been—that I was close to seeing Asmodeus once more.

But it has no effect. Marchosias grunted, "YOU SUMMONED ME LIKE A HUMAN MAGICIAN MIGHT, BUT IN MY OWN REALM. I AM NOT BOUND TO YOU."

"You are bound to Asmodeus," I said brazenly. It let out an unhappy sound, and I cocked my head at it. "You disagree?"

"LAMENT."

It. . .disliked Asmodeus?

It felt like a sin to hear. In my head, I heard church bells ringing, and that old dread welled up in me as if I was heading towards the confessional. Incense clogged my nose, and the eyes of my brethren fell upon me. I feared they could see the truth of my rot and its source. I feared they could all tell.

My face twisted. Marchosias grimaced in response. "OF COURSE THE LORD KNOWS IT," it told me. It had correctly guessed at my horror—the fear I possessed for the sin of blaspheming had transferred from God to Asmodeus. "DO NOT THINK YOU HAVE DECEIVED ME, HUMAN."

As I looked into the golden well of its eyes, I felt dizzy, drawn as if gravity itself had its hands around me. Marchosias showed me, either willingly or otherwise, its past.

This is what I saw:

War.

Long, blond-haired Lucifer Morningstar atop a steed of black, his wings unfurled and glinting in the impossible white of Heaven. His beauty was nearly incomprehensible, every feature carved perfectly, placed there by a master sculptor, but the anger in his eyes undercut his intensity. He appeared more human in that moment, not an untouchable angel. Fury and rage were emotions I could understand. Lucifer Morningstar was full of it, and he wasn't the only one.

Hundreds of angels appeared at his back, all of them divine in appearance, with their smooth skin and long hair and unknowable beauty. All of them appeared humanoid to me, without any of the confusing appearances written in the Bible. These angels attacked with swords and banners raised as humans would. Trumpets rang out. In glimpses, I saw this must have been for my benefit: the truth flickered through, with bodiless orbs of light exploding against one another or metal bands looping around a hundred disembodied eyes locked in battle against beastly amalgamates. That was the truth of the battle and the appearance of the angels. I did not fight when the wool was pulled back over my eyes, much preferring to see the beauty of the angels and the way their muscles tensed with every thrust of their weapons.

I smelled incense and blood, a metallic sweetness cloying the air. Then I saw who must have been Marchosias in amongst the fray. It had long, curly brown hair, brown eyes, a muscular form. I saw the wide-eyed panic, the horror at the sight of blood. I saw its fall with the rest of them. I saw Marchosias' beautiful wings made torn and bloody by the landing. Marchosias let out an awful scream, body bleeding and bruised as it stood, dragging the limp remains of its wings through red earth. And then its body changed, angelic form stripping away as corruption took over and made it as I saw it.

I felt a kinship. Can you blame me? Marchosias had, for whatever reason, denied the Lord, and been punished so fully that its poor body had taken the damage. I felt the pain it had felt, and I knew that it looked at me and saw a pathetic insect of a thing. What could I have said? I would live about as long as a single breath for Marchosias, and I was sure it would hate to be compared to a human.

Still, the image wasn't done. I was imbued with more knowledge: that Heaven had a ranking like Hell had a ranking and that Marchosias had belonged to the Dominion angels, charged with keeping the world in proper order. Marchosias had been tasked with delivering God's justice to the world by being merciful toward human beings. I couldn't quite comprehend how such a benevolent creature had become this, until it showed me.

A series of vignettes filled my mind: Marchosias' life as an angel, the pride it tried and often failed to contain when it succeeded in its duty. Then, the image paused, and a clearer scene emerged. I saw the beautiful angel Lucifer and Marchosias speaking.

"We know that isn't true," Marchosias was saying.

Lucifer, the perfect cosmic creation, said in dulcet tones, "It is what the Lord claims, and it is what we must do."

Marchosias blanched. It bowed as if afraid. "I do not understand. This was not what I was taught. I was made to bring God's justice, but I did not expect to bow before mortal creatures. I did not think I would be called lesser than them. Why does the Lord do this, Samael?"

It was a blasphemous, broken cry. Tears welled in Marchosias' eyes.

Samael, Lucifer, stepped forward to comfort Marchosias, a hand squeezing its shoulder. "Because He intends to subject Himself to the mortal form."

And I saw the vision of the Incarnation, when God would come to Earth as a human, and experience mortal life.

Marchosias was appalled. "Samael—"

"I cannot allow it," Lucifer said. "I see you cannot allow it either. Nothing divine should experience such a thing. I will fight God for His seat, and I will rule this place better than He. Will you fight with me?"

I did not need to see the rest to know Marchosias said yes. But all these memories were tinged with regret!

When my vision cleared, I was still dangling from Marchosias' fingertips. I writhed in its grasp, feeling how small my body was before it. Gasping, I managed, "You wish to return to Heaven?" and I was surprised by how quickly its dark eyes filled with sorrow.

"It is a false hope but one I cling to yet. I wish for heaven to open its arms to me. I wish to return home."

I knew why this Marquis was the one sent to me by Asmodeus. Here was a once religious creature languishing in *regret* at its choice. Would I regret what I had done one day, when the sobering passage of time had stripped away all lustre? After I had been fucked and used and pleasured for lifetimes over lifetimes, would I wake one day, to think, "O! I should have died in that monastery!"

It seemed ridiculous to me at that moment, but I felt I owed something to my old self. I felt I should be sure. So I asked, "What is it that you regret?"

And as Marchosias searched my eyes and thought for an impossibly long moment, I knew it could not name a thing. I knew it wasn't Heaven it lacked, but purpose: that it was hosting festivals and tournaments for entertainment. Marchosias was bored.

I told it: "Heaven gave you a purpose. Direction. Asmodeus has given me a purpose, and with it, my life has changed from dull piety to passion.

Marchosias' eyes flickered. I walked a thin line; it might turn on me at any moment, frustrated by my mortality.

"At the very least, you could put me in my place. You could touch me and fuck me and prove to yourself I am the lowly creature you suspect all humans to be. I want you to use me. Use my flesh for pleasure, and perhaps you will find Heaven there."

Flames burst in its eyes, a hunger that I understood.

"Yes," it said with a slow nod. Its eyes flicked from me to the giants locked in battle. "What will give me pleasure is the truth of humanity's pitiable depravity. Enough friction, and you are pushed into the abyss of orgasm. Contemptible little creatures." I said nothing, but its warm breath, its anger, its general disgust when looking at me—I *was* as depraved as it claimed, and my body twitched, arousal tingling through my cock.

And it ordered, "You are not allowed to orgasm."

I froze. The order itself was tantalising, but it was also—improbable. Not something I could uphold. "What?"

But no answer was given. Marchosias opened its mouth. Cracked lips craned wide and exposed the wide, fat tongue. The giant licked up my body.

My whole lower half grew wet and warm with its saliva. I yelped, bucking at once *away* and *into* the feeling. And this pleased the demon, for it laughed at my distress, and it pinched my wrists slightly harder until I felt the bones of my wrist and forearm strain, the metacarpal crunch and ache. Pain radiated to the tips of my fingers and up my arm, burning even in my shoulder. I couldn't help it: I let out a yelp.

Marchosias chuckled. It grazed my whole torso with the pad of its thumb. My cock bounced from the movement. I kicked the air; I must have looked pathetic, suspended like that, with my cock responding in such a degenerate way. Marchosias spun me and let go of my wrists, gripping my body instead around my waist. My arms dropped heavily, and I gasped, ribs aching from the new pressure. It lowered me down, and I became frightened of being subsumed in the ever-constant light radiating from its groin. The fear overrode all sense. What might give this fallen angel more pleasure: to split me over a cock it lacked or to smite a sinner in the golden light of its nether region? A cruel joke, as befits a demon!

But it did not do anything of the sort. It positioned me gently over its thigh, hand moulding how I sat, how my legs straddled its large thigh, and when it was pleased with this position, it pressed its large forefinger against my back and pushed me down. I folded over and relaxed immediately. My body knew what was coming. My face pressed against curling hairs and warm skin, an early moan curling deep in my chest as my cock twitched towards the warmth. Marchosias grazed my back, thumb large enough to wedge between my cheeks and spread me with one deft motion. Its finger pressed against my hole, nudging between the cheeks like a cockhead. As large as one, if not larger, too.

"F-fuck—"

I expected it to press inside, but it kept one finger close to my hole, and it crept its other hand up my body, stroking over my waist until I was shivering from the stimulation. Its free hand caressed my pointed nipples, and I couldn't help but writhe forward towards the sensation.

Marchosias chuckled.

The full extent of my arousal was a sudden thing. I was rock hard against Marchosias' thigh and grinding desperately in every direction, eager for any kind of pressure.

Marchosias' hands left my nipples. A single finger stroked my head, like I was some pet, and with every touch a starburst of a vision exploded behind my eyes. Marchosias mined my mind for information, for every illicit thought I'd had during my time in the monastery. It rubbed my hole and teased all areas of my body, and at the same time, it called forth humiliating memories, things that had been so shameful I had buried them deep. The memory where my wandering mind had made my cock swell in the middle of a sermon. The memory where I'd taken the confession of a brown, bearded man from the town I was serving, how I had stumbled over my blessing as the thought of his work-hardened body pressing against mine ravaged my attention. I'd thought of his stubble against my balls, the hot tongue sucking gently. I'd imagined him standing up to tower over me, to put me on my knees. I'd been so enamoured with the thought I had almost forgotten to absolve him of his sins.

And then the thoughts changed to the feelings I'd dealt with afterwards. The shame. Or worse: how the shame and the taboo had only made my erection stronger, how I'd fucked my own palm like a desperate slut, rutting up and panting, and only when I'd found that release could I sit with the horror of my mind and what it had conjured.

Now, with Marchosias calling these forth, a flicker of that old shame resurfaced. I couldn't stay focused. The pleasure waned—I felt the blood rushing from my cock to my cheeks —and I tried to press up. Marchosias withdrew its finger from my head and used it to slam my lower back down.

"Where do you think you're going?"

I whimpered. My back ached as it was forced to arch, and the angle forced my face to smash against the warm thigh. Curled hair pushed into my mouth. A smear of saliva dribbled from the corner of my mouth.

Marchosias made a pleased sound and used both its hands to drag my body back along its thigh. It reached around and pressed its index finger to my lips. I licked out with a moan. Its finger pressed against my teeth and gently edged them open, and I allowed it: I opened wide and rocked forward to urge it inside.

It was as wide as a cock, larger than a human's but smaller

than Asmodeus' had been. And so instinct took over. I licked its finger, gentle around the tip like it really was a cock. I pooled more saliva into my mouth and then sank low, stopping before the second knuckle. Marchosias made a sound of approval. I must have looked whorish. Pathetic. I was arched and rubbing my dry cock along its skin, ass spread, and eyes closed, moaning wantonly. It hadn't even fucked me yet.

Marchosias let me work for a few minutes, and then it pinched my sides. I flinched, hands racing down to press uselessly against the forefinger and thumb keeping me still. I barely had time to do much else before Marchosias began fucking my throat. Slowly, at first. No deeper than I had gone myself. Every thrust made it slicker, and when it pushed against the sphincter of my throat, I gagged and convulsed. But I couldn't get away, not with how I was being held. I bucked, struggling. Marchosias only pressed forward until the second knuckle had slipped over my lips.

I went limp.

I focused on breathing. Tears pooled involuntarily in my eyes, and I felt my mouth flood with stringy saliva. Marchosias pulled its finger free, and I felt every ridge of its skin, the bones of its fingers, the sharp tip of its nail drag over my bumped throat and swollen tongue.

I let out a muffled, "*Ah!*"

Marchosias said nothing and made no sound as it pressed that slicked finger back against my hole. I whimpered, and its other hand wrapped around my waist, poised to tear me off its thigh.

"Wait, wait," I mumbled, incoherent. Logically, I knew my body had recovered from its prolapsed state. Even the cuts that proved I had summoned Marchosias were almost nearly healed. But I *feared* to be filled up as intensely.

I was so tense I hadn't realised Marchosias had paused as

I'd asked. I craned around to look at it. Its face was blank, not angry.

Unmoving it said, "It only works if you want it. I do not wish to break you. I wish for you to prove to me you are ruled by your pleasure."

My breathing grew rapid. My eyes flicked down to the finger pressed against me and then back up to the demon's eyes.

"You can't take it?" Marchosias asked. Its tone had shifted—to a teasing, questioning tone. Could I take it? Of course I could. I had taken more! It stroked my head, down my spine. I shivered and arched involuntarily towards its touch, and I felt my hole pucker.

I moaned, head drooping. Why had I bothered to resist? I knew myself too well, and I was the slut Marchosias wanted to see writhing on its fingers. "Fuck me," I said. "*Please*. Stretch me on your fingers. I want—"

But Marchosias knew what I wanted. It pushed forward. Sturdy pressure popped my hole open, the edges wrapping tightly over the demon's nail bed. Marchosias wriggled the tip just slightly, and that was enough for my body to remember. A kind of heat doused my body, an arousal so sudden that I felt my hole open to accommodate more of Marchosias' finger. It did not wait, pressing in over the first knuckle, and from there, it began to move back and forth. All the while, it held my lower half wrapped in its right hand.

"Ah, ah!" I cried out. When I swallowed, I felt that the back of my throat was bruised from the earlier throat fucking. I felt my body tensing; I kept clenching over the width of its finger, hands pressing down against the hold it had around my waist. But nothing I could do would convince it to stop. Marchosias kept making humming noises. The occasional mocking moan would escape its lips seconds after a real one ripped through me. I threw my head back, and that was when the demon repositioned, forcing me to sit upright.

It still held me, allowing me to grow accustomed to the new angle.

But then it let go.

There was nothing beneath my feet. It had dropped me on its finger, and there was nothing I could lean on.

Gravity forced me to slide slowly down onto its finger until the whole thing had impaled me. I whimpered. Pain became pleasure, and then pleasure became too much: the feeling was overwhelming. I jerked to get away—which only made it worse as the finger began to move. My prostate jumped as my cock twitched. Slack-jawed, my head fell back. I gasped. It took its other hand and used one finger to press my chin up ever further. My watery eyes turned to tears as I arched, and gravity made them fall in time with my shuddery breaths.

I was an object, small and portable, and Marchosias was going to use me.

"Fuck yourself," it commanded.

I weakly tried to bounce. The effect was shameful: I ground my hips, thrusting down and up a mere inch before gravity took over.

Fullness filled my belly, and I groaned, gripping my stomach. There, I could feel the bulge of its finger pressing into my guts.

"Fuck. *F-fuck.*"

"As you wish."

A sharp intake of breath. "W—"

Marchosias held me in place, suspended perfectly in the air with my legs flopping about. It slowly dragged its finger all the way out of me, and it popped free with a wet *shlick*. A moment later, it drove back in, just as achingly slow, then out again a fraction faster and in with the same slow, rough force.

And then it threw all caution to the wind and slammed into my ass.

I screamed. Every thrust made me a ragged puppet. All resistance fell away, and the hands I had been using to weakly press against the demon's grip relaxed and slipped limp by my sides.

The only sound was that of slapping skin as its finger crashed into me over and over. I could have cum if it had let me; I felt my prostate throbbing, and my engorged cock was leaking fluid everywhere, droplets spraying with every rough thrust.

But it had told me I couldn't. It had specifically told me not to cum, and if my frustration gave Marchosias pleasure, so bet it—because it gave me pleasure, too. I wanted to be pushed to the edge. I wanted my pleasure held above my head like a reward, not a presumption.

It pulled its finger free, and I crumpled forward with a ragged moan. Saliva fell from my open mouth, and I felt my hole pucker around nothing. Marchosias draped me back over its thigh so I was once against lying down with my back arched. Then, it pressed both its thumbs against my whole. The rest of its hands were pulling me open, making me gape, and like that, it pushed in and pulled both fingers to the side in a stretch.

"*Oh*, fu—" I was gasping, breathing hard. I rocked back and grunted at the sharp pain, and then I was being lifted again. Marchosias was holding me by my ass, thumbs still spreading me wide. I was in a widespread split, upper half dangling, and blood rushed to my head as I slumped forward in the air. Sweat dripped off me, coming to form droplets at the tips of my hair, which fell over my eyes.

"What are you d-doing? Wh—"

Marchosias responded only with a low moan. I felt its hot

breath curling from its throat and over my ass, my balls, my cock. Then, Marchosias' tongue pressed inside.

I cried out, not from pain but from the *warmth* and the *wetness*. The tongue was wide as it lapped up into my insides, turning firm with sudden focus. It fucked forward with intention and then turned wide and soft a moment later.

It ate me with determination. Sometimes Marchosias would slip out and lick up my balls and my cock. Seemingly happy with every desperate buck and thrust, Marchosias did this for minutes until I was insane with want. I reached down between my legs to tug at my swollen cock, but Marchosias pulled its tongue free and hissed at me.

"I'm—I'm sorry—" I gasped, releasing my member. "I won't cum."

It was a promise I wouldn't be able to keep. My body felt electrified, every part hard and poised and ready for release.

Then it flipped me around and—

Took my cock in its mouth

This sensation shocked me. The pleasure was unfocused, not one of those touches where every nerve felt overstimulated, but one where an even bliss throbbed over my body. I couldn't help it. I rolled my hips forward, hands pressed to Marchosias' nose. I had to close my eyes to keep from meeting its large, wide eye, but when it slipped two fingers into my ass and fucked me hard, I snapped them open in shock.

I met the demon's thrilled expression with my brows crushing together and my mouth open for a stream of moans.

"No—no, I'll—"

Marchosias shoved my cock from its lips. The wet, pulsing member flopped against its lips. "Tell me you are slut. Tell me you're worthless, that you're beneath me. That I was right; that Samael and the rest of us were right. All humans are like you. Do this, and you can cum."

"Yes. Yes," I gasped, grinding my hips against nothing but the skin of its lips. It didn't wait for me to prove what I would do and let me slip back inside. I moaned. Pleasure was making me dizzy, but the promise of orgasm focused my mind.

"I'm a whore," I announced in a whisper. Then Marchosias added its tongue, licking up and down furiously, and I cried out, "I'm a *whore!*"

I melted into its mouth. Wetness escaped its lips, saliva coating my whole groin, my lower stomach, my inner thighs. Marchosias moaned with me, eyes eager.

"I'm a slut. I'm such a slut. I'm nothing; I was made for this. I was meant to be used over and over. You were right. I'm not made for anything more than this; all humans are worthless pieces of meat. All of us are beneath you. Oh, Lord, I *can't*—"

I broke off into a rough moan, head thrown back and body limp. Pressure was gathering behind my belly. I rocked forward, head rolling down as I snapped my hips forward, again and again into Marchosias' wet mouth.

"Yes, *yes, yes.*" My hips slapped against its wet lips. "I'm a slut. I'm such a slut, I'm such a slut, I'm—"

Orgasm tore through me. I threw my head back in a silent scream. Marchosias didn't stop, sucking and licking and rocking my body back onto its fingers again and again, and finally, I had to cry out from the feeling. It was too much. Everything was too much. I slumped forward against its nose, dripping and slick and panting.

"I can't," I whimpered. "It's too m—much—!"

Marchosias tore its fingers out of me—I yelled—and placed me on my back, draped over its thigh. I panted, my deflating cock leaking over my thigh and onto Marchosias. I lay there for so long I might have fallen asleep. The pleasure had exhausted me.

Marchosias ran a single wide finger down my body. I shivered and opened my arms.

It looked down at me with a soft smile. "THERE IS NO HEAVEN NEITHER YOU NOR I ARE GETTING INTO. BUT AT THE VERY LEAST, I CAN BE CERTAIN I MADE THE RIGHT DECISION ALL THOSE MILLENNIA AGO."

I said nothing, though I possessed the urge to be witty. I did not wish to move; I could see myself being tempted by Marchosias into staying.

"I must find Asmodeus," I said, rolling over and pushing up, though my arms shook.

When I stood shakily on Marchosias' thigh, thunderous applause erupted before us. I squinted against the light and saw all of Marchosias' tournament had given up their battle to witness my destruction. The two giants were roaring and clapping wildly. The imps leapt in the air, and the lesser demons cheered for my display. I shivered and glanced away with shyness, but Marchosias cooed and gently nudged my head back toward them.

It said, "YOU HAVE PROVEN TO THEM THAT THEY WERE RIGHT, TOO. FAITH CAN ALWAYS BE SHAKEN, MOST ESPECIALLY AFTER SO MUCH TIME." Marchosias' hot breath curled over my neck. "HEAVEN IS NOT WORTH IT. WE WILL CELEBRATE *HERE!*"

It roared, and the cheer was answered. The whole arena lit up with joyous celebration. Marchosias grabbed me and stood, hefting my still recovering body in the air. It put me up on its shoulder.

"WHAT IS NEXT FOR THE HUMAN?" it asked me.

"I need to find a Prince of Hell," I said, and it nodded.

It brought forefinger and thumb to its lips and whistled shrilly. A cry sounded from the air, and two bobbing shapes moved ever closer. Not imps, though.

But cherubim!

The strange creatures that had previously flown away were back, their many heads swivelling in interest, four sets of eyes boring through me. They flew close, and I knew what to do, stretching out my arms for them to grasp. They latched, and I was pulled off Marchosias' back. All the weight of my body strained against the sockets of my shoulders, but I did not mind the pain.

I craned back to look at Marchosias as we departed. It stood and unfurled its beautiful wings, and I heard trumpets start up again, all their discordance stripped away, so they sounded nearly heavenly.

❧   4   ❧

I somehow slept whilst the cherubim transported me, and by the time I had awoken, they were long gone.

I opened my eyes to find I was horizontal once more, asleep atop a bed of grass and tiny black flowers whose petals were long and wet.

I peeled myself from the ground, groggy with exhaustion. A circular castle tore through the sky, the red haze of the horizon forming a halo glow around the sharp black edges of the jagged structure. It was unlike the castle occupied by Malphas, which had appeared oily and deeply inhuman. This seemed familiar and human. It looked to be carved from a black sandstone, and it had a great many banners flying from its turrets. A castle wall surrounded the central keep, and it rose out of a hillside that abruptly ended in a cliff, a natural defence, as one would expect across much of Europe.

A crowd had gathered. Demons and hags and all manner of creatures danced around maypoles at its base. I walked closer until I became part of this crowd, and no one paid me any mind. They were cheering. They cried out, "For the great Prince Vassago! We bless him! We bless him!"

The cheers were oddly genuine, and they seemed out of place in Hell until I considered the hierarchy of Earth seemed apparent in both Hell and Heaven.

The hags I recognised as the same type who had fed me the flower—the food of Hell—and I approached them with ease. Perhaps I should have felt fear, should have quaked to approach such a creature, with its long nails and stringy hair. But she turned as if to greet an old friend and cried out in excitement, reaching out as I approached. When I was close enough, she grazed those nails over my flesh and said, "You are the one my sisters spoke of! You are the one here for King Asmodeus! You are the one!"

She took me by the wrist, fingers long enough to wrap easily around the join, and she pulled me through the crowd. I guessed there were about a hundred demons in attendance of various lesser ranks, though I could only guess at their functions in Hell and in the kingdom of this Prince. Ribbons streamed from the maypoles in bright colours, and those same black flowers dotted the grey-green grass. The joy was infectious. My heart began to race as we picked our way through the dancing crowd. I must have smelled enough like Hell not to offend anyone's noses, for no one looked to me except to smile and grin and say *Vassago,* a name spoken like a prayer, like a greeting or an oath. Everything smelled like spices and amber, and I did not mind that my body touched that of many demons. There was nothing sexual about those instances: it was the first time my naked body had been touched platonically. The first time my nakedness sparked not even a hint of shame in my mind.

When we burst from the crowd, the hag let go of my arm and gripped her skirts with both hands. She hefted them high to expose two mottled shins, and she climbed up a rocky incline balanced against the black stone of the keep's wall. There, she turned and exclaimed loudly, "Have faith, all ye! A human has descended into Hell by choice, here to please our Lords, here in proof of humanity's true nature! Celebrate him and rejoice!"

The demons in the crowd cheered for me and only doubled when she added, "He was once a priest! Now, he has forsaken God entirely to dedicate himself to this place! My sisters have said so!"

The joy became too much. Many large demons dropped their maypole ribbons and ran for me. With grace, they plucked me from the ground and hefted me high above their heads. Great clawed hands took care not to pierce my skin, and a hundred voices came together to beseech the Prince for his attention.

"A guest for Prince Vassago! A guest for Prince Vassago!"

The chant floated up the way I had once imagined prayers would, only this time, the pleading was answered. A crack sounded from high above, and we all craned up to see a window had been opened from the keep. The distance meant we could see nothing but shadow, and even then, the window was roughly pulled shut. Moments later, another window opened from the turret—a strange sight, for it appeared like a cube of stone simply vanished, replaced by impenetrable blackness. From this darkness emerged a ladder made of rope and wooden panels. A primitive thing, well-worn and fraying. It dropped quickly, the panels clattering against the stone, and I realised belatedly there were no visible doors to this Prince Vassago's keep. There was no point of entry save for this rope, and even then, it did not descend all the way.

The demons around me cheered. I could feel their swell, and I craned to look as a sea of reaching, leathery hands popped up from the crowd. They were pushing me upwards, helping me reach the end of the ladder. I gained control of my senses and scrambled to grasp the rope.

I will say this of that moment: I thought of brotherhood. I know it is strange, and I know it seems like very little happened, but for a man whose entire life was spent in service to an institution built upon such kindness, whose institution had failed him, whose brothers had been closer to watchful spies than family—to have a taste of a community, however strange or beastly, filled my poor empty heart.

I took hold of the ladder and lurched as my body weight shifted, but I climbed with purpose, even as my limbs shook and the flimsy ladder wobbled beneath my weight. I gazed up and saw impish faces peering out at me from the dark. Abruptly, their heads swivelled back into the hole and then back out again to me, and it was as if they had received an order, for they began to heave the ladder up with me braced and clutching.

Moments later, I reached for the dark, and their tiny hands wrapped around my arms and pulled me into the turret. Pitch black greeted me. The hole I had climbed through opened into a dark tunnel. The smell of mildew clogged my nose, but I scarcely minded it. I leaned out of the hole and waved down to the gathered crowd of demons, who leapt up in joy at the sight of me; I thought blasphemous things about the Saviour and thought to compare myself to him. I felt greed and a new lust fill my heart. Could I be a messiah to this realm? Or would I always be an elevated pet?

Many demons, like Marchosias, only enjoyed my presence for the proof of human depravity I brought with me.

"Come," a rough voice prompted. The imps were staring at me, their golden beady eyes the only things I could see in the dark. The wet slapping of feet guided me. I followed along helplessly, feeling dog-like in how I trailed. Occasionally, light split through a seam in the stone, and I could see the tunnel was as I expected—stone and empty, meant for these creatures to walk through. As such, the ceiling began to lower, and soon, I was forced to squat and crawl if I were to continue following them. Seeing me on my knees gave the creatures joy. A chittering laughter started up as soon as I went down, and one of the imps began to pet my head as if I truly were a dog.

"Good boy," it told me. A flash of light revealed its yellowed teeth, filed to sharp points, a smile splitting its face wide. The impish head sat atop a stout body with leathery brown wings and a forked tail, only unlike the other imps I had seen in this realm, this one wore—finery.

I blinked. Darkness enveloped us again, and I crawled awkwardly forward, wincing as the cold stone roughened my knees. At the next seam, the light showed me I had been right. All the imps were dressed, wearing simple short surcoats in cream and embellished with black. The sight was absurd! More than anything, seeing their clothed bodies made me anxious. Hell had been separated from Earthly ways.

What kind of demon was I to meet next?

As I wondered this, I heard a rumbling growl echo in my ears. I went rigid, waiting in the dark. The imps continued forward, little feet stomping on the stone, but I blocked them out and strained to listen.

"Asmodeus?" I said aloud.

Abruptly, the imps stopped. They looked back at me and said nothing.

I closed my eyes to avoid seeing their impish eyes, and I said again, "My Lord?"

An appreciative sound as slow and deep as rolling thunder crackled across my senses. I felt Asmodeus abruptly, there like lightning, and I gasped that I could feel it near me.

"You look good like that, little priest."

"W-what?"

"On your knees, skin red and scraped. You look good crawling

towards what you want. It is a natural state for you: you waited not at all to go down."

I swallowed. "You are watching."

Not a question: a statement. A hurried, near-nervous statement.

Asmodeus replied in that same sultry tone: *"Are you pleased that I watch you?"*

What could I say? Of course I was pleased! But if I were to voice this to Asmodeus, Prince of Lust, a King of Hell—I foresaw a punishment waiting, a destruction of my ego. The last time we had spoken, I had breached an unspoken contract. I had asked Asmodeus if it would pleasure me when I was next in its presence.

"I do not know what to say, my Lord," I mumbled, which was the truth. I shook frightened in the tunnel, and I did not know what I could say that would please Asmodeus. I feared it as much as I loved it—and that had always been my relationship with things I worshipped.

As if hearing me, Asmodeus' growl began again.

"Are you my slut?"

I needed no time to think. I shivered and said, "Yes," and something about admitting this calmed my nerves.

"My good little lamb?"

"Yes."

"Are you learning what pleases you, Alessandro?"

I exhaled noisily. "It pleases me to crawl for you."

A laugh, deep and happy. *"Does it?"*

"Yes."

A moment passed where Asmodeus said nothing, and I assumed it had grown bored with our chat. But then, almost as quiet as a whisper, it said to me: *"I watched you with the Marquis Marchosias. I watched you squirm and bounce and moan. I watched orgasm tear through your body. Are you closer to knowing yourself now?"*

"Yes," I said, though I was flushed. And then, somewhat brazenly, "Are you teasing me, my Lord?"

A very deep and serious, "*Always.*"

I slumped back on my haunches, not understanding. "Have I done something wrong?"

"*No, little priest. Not at all. You questioned me, and I questioned myself. For I am not like God, who will take no criticisms and will smite any He does not favour. You are right: you cannot be wholly mine if you are not wholly yours first. You are still the Church's child in many ways. You are good at being fucked, but you find it difficult to be pleasured. Yet you try—you try to be good for me.*"

I swallowed. My head buzzed with the praise.

"*I want you to focus now. I want you to be good for me. I want you to please my Prince and my Duke, and I want you to come to me willing, with all your qualms quelled, and all your past wiped clean.*"

I frowned. "What do you mean?"

"*You have struggled with your pleasure. I want you to fight that struggle. And so, I do not want you to fuck the Prince. I want you to make love to the Prince.*"

I blanched. "I don't—"

"*I want you to look into its eyes, and give more than your body, for I want you to do the same to me. I want all of you, little priest. No part of your body, your mind, or your soul should remain thinking of Earth or of Heaven. I see in your head the young man you fantasise of.*"

Shocked, I realised it was speaking of Oliviero!

"*I see the regrets you hold for your unmet desires. You may solve this with the Duke, but for the Prince, you must solve your worry. Be vulnerable. Be fully naked for him, Alessandro.*"

And I was horrified by this, full of despair and embarrassment. It was so much worse than splitting my hole over a demon's fingers, or letting a *centaur* enter me. It was the feeling I had encountered when those lesser demons had put their mouth on my cock and my hole, when Furfur had touched me for my own pleasure. But the vulnerability I had felt then had been nothing compared to how I would feel under a truly loving touch.

I shivered. I said, "Yes, my Lord," and waited for Asmodeus' final remarks. They never came.

I knew what I had to do, but I was terrified.

‹ 5 ›

By the time I had emerged from the tunnel, my body ached. My knees bore the most damage; the caps were red-raw and bruised. Indents scooped into my palms and dirt covered all limbs. The coolness of the tunnel had given me goosebumps, but the keep itself was warm, and a fine sheen of sweat had begun on my lower back.

The keep was very fine and very *human* in design. I went rigid just being in there. My body stiffened on impulse, and I felt shamed for my nudeness—which I realised was the point of this place's design. After Asmodeus' insight, I understood better that my wantonness was a state I could achieve, one that fell behind a wall of fog whenever I was reminded of my humanity or my once-faith. Anything close to human made it more difficult for me. I wondered vaguely if the monstrous bodies of my lovers so far had allowed me to be free with them.

The imps walked me forward through lustrous corridors that seemed to go on endlessly. The walls were decorated with all manner of art or hanging bronze armour, and again, the art appeared human. Painted portraits of unknown nobility lined the walls, and much was in a style I recognised as Italian. This might have been an amalgamated castle, with influences from across Europe, but I could imagine it most suited to Italy. I could imagine in that moment that I was still a priest, summoned to take a final confession, or bestow last rites upon a wealthy lord.

The imps' surcoats flapped as they moved. In this light, I could better see the designs they bore, which was a sigil like the many I had laid before during my time in Hell.

Indeed, the room they brought me into was a large bedroom, fit with a four-poster bed, a swooning sofa, a desk, a carpet, and a large expanse of floor before the door. On that wooden floor, the sigil sat etched.

ONCE I WAS INSIDE, the imps closed the door without a word, and I was left to my own devices.

Usually, I would have gone to my knees and fumbled with some blade or another to bleed into the sigil and summon the next demon with speed. But here I hesitated.

I was frightened, you see. More frightened than I had been for any of the demons. The false bravado I'd possessed for Marchosias seemed a distant dream. If all I had to do was bend over and take whatever this Vassago wanted to do to me, I would!

But the thought of looking in his eyes as he touched me, fingers trailing over my skin, kisses soft, thrusts slow—my stomach rioted!

I sat down on the swooning sofa and put my head in my hands, and when that did naught to calm me, I shot up and began to pace the room. I opened the closets expecting to find them empty but instead found them brimming with clothing. All manner of tunics and fanciful clothes burst free. I closed the wardrobe and walked next to the desk, which had papers written in some infernal language I could not understand, though the occasional word became familiar the longer I stared at it. I could read "*Vassago, Prince of Hell*" and "*the good-natured prince*" as terms that occurred excessively throughout the letter. Besides the letters was a sharp letter opener and a leather-bound journal. I left the letter opener for later and unwrapped the book, which was a sketchbook.

And in it, there were drawings of me.

As realistic as the most precise portrait, these drawings showed me in every stage of my descent into Hell. Some showed me in my cassock, or with my clerical collar, or on my knees glistening with the fluids of other creatures. They showed me wanton and desperate and alive, and all of them were drawn with great care.

Perhaps with affection.

I dropped the leather-bound book and stepped back from the table. My heart raced—not because I had been watched by this Prince, nor that it seemed to have captured every blemish and detail of my body, but because of that affection.

I had two choices: stand here in fear eternally or turn around and face this demon. In a moment of immense bravery, I wrenched the letter opener from the table, stalked to the sigil, and slit open my palm as I had done so many times before. My stomach lurched as the blood dripped to the ground. I did all this standing without my usual reverence; I stripped the sacrosanct from the ritual. I felt too nervous to bow, too shaken to show much deference in that moment. The sigil shone a bright gold, and an answering rumble shook the castle. Then: silence.

I waited, poised in eerie stillness. Time conspired with my anxiety to weaken what little confidence I had remaining in my body, and it became impossible to watch the door at all. I turned with embarrassment burning my face and stumbled back to the desk, where I carefully replaced the letter opener and waited for the wound in my hand to knit itself up.

It didn't.

The door creaked open, and I spun to face Prince Vassago.

And *he* was not what I expected.

Vassago appeared as I would imagine any beautiful human prince. His eyes were warm, and crows-feet pulled the skin around his eyes towards a look of eternal amusement. In fact, all the lines on his face suggested human emotion: smile lines at his cheeks and across his forehead. He looked like he might have been from Italy, like an emperor of the Holy Roman Emperor, possessing that dark raven colour in his hair and the warmth in his skin. He had a dazzling, wide smile that he flashed at me immediately, and his eyes were a warm brown struck through with amber. His hair was slicked away from his face with a moustache that curled at the sides. Beautiful sapphire earrings dangled from his lobes. The Prince dressed in a heavy, fur-lined cape with a stunning blue velvet doublet with gold buttons and decorations. A lopsided hat draped over his head, and red-and-white feathers burst from the right side. Underneath it all, Prince Vassago still smiled that dazzling, welcoming smile.

"Oh, pardon me!" he said, and his voice had a honey warmth to it. Jovially, Vassago swung his arms out and walked across the threshold. The door closed gently behind him without so much as a wave towards it.

Vassago's eyes flashed to me and then to my hand, which I held away from my body. Droplets of blood were gathering at my feet.

"Well, that won't do, will it?" he murmured, still smiling. "Come, Alessandro. Come and sit!"

He took me very gently by the forearm. Beneath his touch, my body was as brittle as a sheet of ice and just as cold. I walked where he directed me, and I sat on the waiting bed, arm resting in his lap.

"Are you alright?" the Prince asked me.

I had said nothing, though I felt the blood had drained from my face. How alright could I be about being treated with kindness by a demon? I couldn't trust it.

I said eventually, "You know my name?"

"Oh, yes." His hand dashed into his tunic, and from it, he pulled free a missive, which he waved at me, the thick parchment warbling from the movement. "Our King Asmodeus Itself has warned me of your approach. You've been quite exceptional so far, haven't you?"

"*Warned* you?" I picked my words carefully, but I couldn't help but snag on that.

A warm smile bloomed beneath Vassago's moustache. No hint of malice clouded its eyes. "That's right. I do believe we have a lot of work to cover. Why don't I take my clothes off?"

Vassago began to stand, and my stomach dropped. "It doesn't have to be. A lot of work, I mean. If you were to use me as you saw fit, then I—"

"Well, it's not about *using*, is it?" Vassago freed himself from his fur-lined cape. It fell to the ground in a heavy heap. Vassago looked at me, brown eyes narrowing. "I was told you wanted to be pleasured. That you were brazen enough to petition Asmodeus for reciprocal touch. Have I been misinformed?"

I shook my head and told him the truth. It all came out in one great rush. I sat there naked, exposed on the bed, feeling that everything was far too human and familiar for me to be acting as I was. At any moment, I feared someone I knew might walk through those doors and see me. I feared everything had been a dream, and I would wake in the monastery alone and untouched for eternity.

"I'm frightened of such a touch. I had a moment of lucidity, I believe: a blip where I knew the best whore for Asmodeus would be a man who knows his own pleasure, his own body, that it might be used by the Prince of Lust more intentionally. I am doing this because Lord Asmodeus saved my life. The least I can do is ensure a human is perfectly settled to their new role."

Vassago barely shifted. "*What* type of touch frightens you?"

And I said, "A loving one."

Vassago's fingers moved to pop the first three buttons of his doublet open. The tan flesh beneath burst with black chest hair. He held my gaze and gently lifted my chin with his finger. Vassago's face drew very close. Raspberries and cinnamon, his scent was. . .far too sweet for a demon.

And he asked me: "Do you want to be *raped*, Alessandro?"

I jolted back away from his touch, but I held his gaze, and without thinking, I had a dozen visions flooding my weak mind. I imagined Vassago with his hands around my throat. I imagined kicking weakly as his strength picked me up, and turned me, and held me down. His weight would crush me into the mattress of this bed, and in amongst its soft sheets and pillows, I could hide my face. How much easier would it be to cry out if I had the excuse of pain? I could hide my desire and justify my shame in the one act; a facsimile of rape meant to shield me from my own fears.

Cold doused me.

Is that what I had been doing all this time? I had opened myself immediately to rough, violent fucking, and yet I grew frightened by the thought of sweet touches. That intimacy was far worse than the intimacy of giving my body over to be used.

Vassago was saying, "It's a fantasy I wouldn't be averse to indulging, but it would only be a fantasy. I enjoy consent the most."

I blinked at him, and likely, he could see or smell my fear. Vassago sat back down beside me and took my bleeding hand in both of his. The warmth from his touch made my heart race.

"What is it that *you* want, Alessandro?"

I fought the urge to claim I didn't know what I wanted. I closed my eyes and thought and sat with the uncomfortable dread pooling in my belly. I wanted to be had and used and fucked to the point of oblivion. At the same time, I wanted to be taken care of and treated kindly—even if this frightened me.

I told Vassago, "I want to. . . I want to be able to enjoy myself. I want to feel pleasure. I enjoy being told what to do, but I also wish I knew—what *I* wanted for myself."

Vassago waited in silence, and I dredged up more things to tell it.

"I've never. . ." I flushed to the point my cheeks hurt with their burn. "Why does this feel so horrible?"

Vassago made a low, soft noise and dragged its hands away from my own. His fingers grazed my palm, and not even an ounce of pain flared beneath the touch: the wound was healed. Vassago reached up and placed his hand upon my cheek, thumbing gently at my face. It was hard to look at him. It was the hardest thing I'd ever done.

"Hidden secrets reside in your subconscious," he whispered. "Why don't we look?"

Vassago knocked our foreheads together. His breath mingled with mine. When I opened my eyes, I hoped he would be looking at me—but he wasn't. His eyes were closed, one hand holding our heads together and the other resting gently on the bed. I was brave. I slipped my finger into his and jolted when he squeezed back.

Then, I felt him rummaging. He used no fingers, but a fuzziness overwhelmed my focus. I groaned as vertigo attacked my senses, and Vassago slipped his other hand free of mine to steady my head.

"Calm," he cooed, but his voice was a distant fog. I was enveloped by something more, and soon, my consciousness had faded entirely.

❧ 6 ❧

Be devoted to one another in brotherly love; give preference to one another in honour.

ROMANS 10

WE WORK IN SILENCE.

It is a nightly occurrence: from sunset until morning, we choose not to speak to one another—an order meant to focus us on our work.

Silence is the bane of my existence, for it is within these quiet hours that I find my mind most unruly. It is far easier to stare at my brothers and have the excuse of staring for their attention, and not for ungodly reasons. But so, too, do I find that, without the distraction of conversation, I think over and over again about why God has punished me so.

I am choir monk Alessandro, twenty-two and not yet a don. I am working not in the monastery I was raised, but in a small town I have visited in the south of Italy. The details do not matter: the boy does.

He is three years older than me, and brilliant. His name is Raffiano, but he wishes to be called Paul. Paul is beautiful. I see Heaven in his eyes, God in that perfect smile. He is kind, and I cannot comprehend what his kindness means. If it means anything at all.

One day, I reach out and I take his hand. He squeezes my hand back. I think to myself that this is it. I have been vulnerable; I have done the thing I have been scared to do, and for as long as the silence lasts, I don't have to know whether Paul sees it that way or not.

The next day, I am still delusional with my love for him. He tells me, "It is good to have a brother unafraid of his affections. You are Romans 10 in a man, Alessandro. I aspire to be like you."

And he will still take my hand for the next month, but I know I am a brother to him. When I leave the town and return to my own monastery, he writes me a letter with Romans 10 written below his farewell.

I do not reply.

❦

I SNAPPED awake in Prince Vassago's arms and squirmed with fear as I attempted to sit up. My head aches, and Vassago is shushing me. My cheeks are wet with tears.

Paul. Raffiano. I hadn't thought about him in years.

"You wanted affection, then. Not sex."

"All of it," I whispered.

"Perhaps it became easier for you to think of carnal sin as more accessible than for one of your brethren to return your affections."

I hated that Vassago could speak so easily on this. I hated that I might be eternally craving something I couldn't have. I wanted to ask about the Hellish visions I had been shown of my monastery. I imagined Oliviero on his knees, my rosary in his mouth. I squeezed my eyes shut; it was easy to think of Oliviero like that. If he had looked at me with care in his eyes, would I have found the will to put my cock in his mouth?

Vassago shushed me; I had been breathing hard. He ran his fingers through my hair and encouraged me to lie back again. His touches were soft, gentle strokes across my neck or my chest, and never lower.

"Alessandro. You want to be loved."

"Is it a sin?"

"We don't care about that here."

But Vassago wasn't comprehending. I *wanted* love to be a sin. It would be so much easier for a demon to indulge in affection if it was against the will of God.

I said, "What if I have condemned myself to an eternity where I will never be loved?"

And Vassago said, with great wisdom, "Why are you worried about that when you are currently unable to let yourself love at all?"

I turned to look at it, relaxing minutely under its gaze. To shift the conversation away from such vulnerable things, I asked, "You're... benevolent?"

"I am good-natured," Vassago corrected. "Still a demon."

I nodded, though I didn't fully understand. Vassago smiled. "I am perhaps the most honest of all my brethren. I have no interest in trickery. I encourage true natures to emerge."

"Is that all?" I whispered quite cynically.

Vassago ignored my tone. "No, no. I share the past and future with any who summon me, should they ask. I can locate lost objects, or—"

"Tell me my future," I said quickly.

Vassago looked at me, a devious little smile spilling onto his lips. "What would you know?"

"If I'm happy one day. Loved." I glanced away, ashamed that I was so desperate to hear these words.

But the demon only took my face between its fingers and said, "If you allow me to kiss you, if you let me be slow and gentle with you, if you tell me what you like and dislike, then I can see a future where you have all those things and more."

I nodded, and he let go of me. I thought he would lean in then and there, but he seemed to know better. After that moment, Vassago spent hours talking to me, touching me. He made me laugh. He showed me his time in Heaven, the way Marchosias had done. The outrage he had felt at his creator subjecting Himself to a mortal life, the lack of understanding he'd had for God's decision, and his refusal to accept it. It all seemed—well, rather justified. How odd it was to me that these demons had not been as cruel as the ones occupying inferior ranks.

Vassago knew so much of what I had studied because he had lived it.

As we talked and laughed, I felt as I had done around Paul: that affection for another who understands you.

I know it was likely magic. I know it *must* have been, to make any sense at all. I might have been lying draped across Vassago's bed for days or months, a slow romance blooming in mere seconds of my consciousness; Hell was Hell. It followed no rules. In any case, I felt affection, attraction, and equal parts fear and desire every time I met Vassago's eye.

This time, when he shuffled closer, I did not flinch away. He smelled as familiar as myself, and all my walls lessened until he had wrapped his arm around my back and pulled me close. Vassago leaned his mouth down, and I surged up to meet him. We breathed each other in, and then I was fighting to tear his doublet free.

And he stopped me.

"I'm meant to be making *love* to you. Not fucking you senseless."

My gut churned in fear, and I let go of him immediately.

He was chiding me, and it felt as terrifying as a lecture from a bishop. Vassago took my hand in his and guided it back to touch him.

"Slow," was all he said, murmured softly like a reminder. He kissed my cheek and then my neck.

My nerves were shot. I jerked at every touch, terrified and yet wanting. Vassago ignored my mewls of fear, and soon, he was pulling moans from my lips. He moved slowly, tongue lapping up my neck, lips sucking on my earlobe as his fingers trailed down my waist. He tongued at my nipples, entire mouth pressed to the perked bud, and I rolled my hips instinctively, eager for him to remove my pants.

I was growing hard, face flung to the side and eyes closed, when Vassago tilted my chin back towards him and commanded, "Open your eyes, Alessandro."

I squeezed even tighter before I gained the courage, and then I was staring up into the warm brown eyes of a man I felt some kind of love for. A man I was certain loved me back.

The absurdity of the situation meant nothing to me. I wasn't thinking about how it was possible or moral. I was thinking: Prince Vassago loves me, and I am terrified of that love. Prince Vassago loves me, and I *crave* that love.

He kissed me gently on the lips, and then his kisses became slow and intentional. Tongue licked out against my lips, and I opened my mouth for him with a soft moan. Vassago shifted himself so he was straddling both my hips with his legs. He undressed himself above me, unbuttoning his doublet slowly, peeling it over his head with inefficient motions designed to tease. With the blue fabric removed, my eyes were filled with the pillowed rise of his pectorals and the sea of black hair that curled over his bare skin. He arched slightly; I'd never seen a man so muscular arch in this way. I reached out to touch him. His thighs and ass were warm in the cream hose, and my cock twitched towards their soft centre, the cleft between the two cheeks. Vassago lowered himself onto me with a knowing laugh.

"Do you want to put it in me?" he asked, looking down at me.

And I—laughed. It was a panicked sound. I gripped both his thighs and tried to throw him off me, but the Prince was far stronger, and he stayed fixed in silence, waiting for my panic to subside.

He was being serious. This demon was requesting of me something I had never done.

"I. . .I've never. . ."

"Make love to me, Alessandro," he whispered, bending low for another kiss. He stayed pressed to my mouth, inhaling hard, and when he pulled away, his hands were against my cheeks, eyes searching.

Waiting for my answer, for my acquiescence. I gasped, drawing in all the air in the world for my answer, but I couldn't even say it. I nodded my head, and a small smile appeared on Vassago's face.

He moved down my body slowly, the way Furfur had done, fingers dancing in the soft divots of my groin to tease the tender flesh. He put his tongue on my balls and sucked gently at them, the underside of his tongue lapping up the full hot length of my cock, which was aching. He sucked at the head teasingly, slowly, a great wash of saliva coating my cock, and pleasure was a mounting thing. The rough hairs of his moustache tickled against the sensitive skin, a gentle scrape that had me bucking up into the warm embrace of his mouth.

Vassago gagged and spluttered, sounds he followed up with moaning and a firm but encouraging grip on my hips. He worked me with his mouth, up and down, and often would gag himself for my own pleasure; the tip of my cock kissed the back of his throat, and I could feel every time the sphincter of it pulsed around my length.

Seconds turned to minutes, and then I was in a dream-like trance with a wash of pleasure encompassing me every time I rolled my hips. It was easy when he was down there to forget I was meant to be making love; I could fuck the warm, wet vestibule without worry. So when he pulled free with a grunt and brought himself up again to be kissed, I grew anxious once more. He was hard himself, and we turned to lie face to face so we might fondle one another and kiss and stare, a ritual of a kind that slowly unstitched my worry from this growing tapestry of touch.

Vassago's beard grazed against my clean-shaven face. I drew him closer and breathed deep, inhaling his scent, and a valve opened in my body: a flood of warmth as blood surged into my already aching cock. Vassago noticed. He smiled against my lips and reached down to squeeze around the member, tugging carefully and teasingly as I spread my legs for his touch.

"What do you want?" he whispered, and I thought of Asmodeus at my first summoning. The answer I had given then had been *you*, but it seemed insubstantial now. I wanted something precise.

I closed my eyes and thought back to the decades of fantasies I had entertained in the monastery. They came to me in ill-formed flashes. Most of them had been nothing more than picturing my fellow brethren naked, and it had been years before those simple sins lost their flavour. When I'd wanted to access the same thrill I had felt in those early days, I thought of greater taboos: of someone's hand edging up my cassock in the middle of a sermon or something surging towards me when I was bent over in the garden pulling out the weeds strangling my beautiful flowers. And then the fantasies had become more specific.

Oliviero spread on my bed, back arched and looking back at me; a lustful stare framed by long lashes, face shadowed by lust. I imagined the swell of his balls, the sharp angles of his hips, and how the meat of his thighs might spread as he settled into the bed.

It had been a fantasy that seemed most inaccessible. Looking back, I could understand why so many of my desires had focused on my body as the object of fucking. It seemed easier to comprehend myself as a vessel to be used by other's desires, and it kept my own desires safely locked behind a door of deniability. If I was used, it didn't mean I *wanted* to be used.

But to direct Vassago now would confirm what I had always known: I was whorish in every conceivable way. I wanted to enjoy the bodies of men as much as I wanted to be enjoyed. I realised I could desire both: that even if, in my heart, I was most drawn to being taken, I did desire to give on occasion.

And such an occasion was now.

"I want you on your knees," I whispered. Vassago let go of me and shifted. He removed his hose, and the mattress creaked as he changed positions, and then he was lying with his face pressed into the pillow and his knees tucked beneath his hips. He was arching, chest pressed to the mattress. I shivered and pushed off the bed to see better.

Vassago's was all perfect angles and curves bent over the bed like that. His ass was firm and round, and the muscle of his hamstrings was evident, tiny black hairs curling sparsely along the skin. I couldn't see much of his head from this angle, just the rush of black hair obscured by the curve of his upper back. My eyes were transfixed on the heavy droop of his balls, which fell so perfectly I was transfixed by the sight of them. I reached out and cupped them. Vassago leaned back into the touch with a shiver, his cock straining hard. I ran my fingers over his back and over his ass, and I watched the twitch of his hole as my breath rushed over it.

I got off on the bed, lowered myself, and pressed my face between the cheeks.

Now, this felt like the most dutiful of all acts I had partaken in. I was on my knees off the bed, the way I would be in prayer, my hands clasped either side of Vassago's cheeks to spread them apart. My tongue lapped over his balls, up his taint, over his hole, tentative and unsure, until Vassago pressed back with a moan and another blockade lifted from my mind. I buried my face eagerly between his cheeks and licked like it was my duty, tonguing up and down and around the hole as deep, breathy moans filled the room. Vassago's hole kept twitching closed, and I pressed my tongue against it, wanting to fuck it open. My tongue lacked the strength.

Frustrated, I reached around to fondle Vassago's cock, slowly stroking over the slick tip, just as I pressed my thumb to Vassago's ass. I pressed hard, and it slipped inside with a pop.

"*God*," Vassago heaved, a false prayer that made me whine loudly.

"What of Him?" I whispered back, understanding perhaps for the first time the sadistic pull the demons felt whenever they saw me desperate like this; a religious man overrun by lust.

Vassago began to rock back and forth on his knees. My finger popped free of his wet hole with a *shlick*, and again and again, Vassago rutted back onto it with a grunt. I tore my finger free at the next rock backwards and delighted in Vassago's rough cry. His pink hole twitched, small gape quivering, and then I drove forward again with my tongue. This time, I had no trouble slipping in. I flexed my tongue and pushed it deep, and when that began to make my jaw ache, I rocked my head back and forth, fucking in and out of Vassago's ass until it was warm, wet, and open.

Vassago arched into it, thrusting down to meet my tongue

and moaning loudly. He pushed himself off the pillow for a better vantage, and his wordless cries became a "*Yes, yes, yes,*" percussive and deliberate.

Saliva ran down my chin, and my own moans filled the room, and I thought of the perfection of this design: of how much *fun* I was having, of Vassago's beauty, of the way we fit together. I found what I wanted wasn't always total domination. I wanted to give and to receive. I wanted a symbiosis of pleasure, an understanding I could reach with each partner.

So when Vassago said, "I want you inside me," I pulled my tongue free and urged him onto his back.

In any other instance, I would have wanted a man—a demon—like Vassago inside of me. But I couldn't deny the urge I had to feel the depth of him.

"Alessandro. *Alessandro*," Vassago hissed. He looked back at me over his shoulder, dark hair covering one eye. His mouth hung open as he panted. "Touch me. Come now; I want you to fuck me."

His head pushed back into the pillow, and I was thrilled by the excitement driving him to move so eagerly. He looked beautiful on his back.

"Hold your legs apart."

He shifted and held his beautiful legs. Brown eyes framed by thick brows and curled hair. Hair covered his chest, belly, arms, legs. I ran my fingers over his feet, which were smooth and bare, and I came close to him. Our cocks were straining. I looked at his ass, relaxed enough I could see it pulsing. I wanted to press inside, but I stopped myself. I leaned down to kiss Vassago slowly instead. He moaned and rolled his hips high. Our bodies touched, hips meeting, the bones of our pelvises locking together as if our bodies were a shattered mosaic being pieced back together. Vassago's fingers laced into my hair and tried to pull me closer, but I resisted. I pulled away and looked down at him, and said, "I am nervous."

I expected a flicker of disdain to pass over his face, but nothing of the sort happened. I could forget what he was and where we were because he sat up, took my hand, and pressed it to his belly. I felt the warmth of the skin, the slight softness of the flesh.

"We are two men loving one another. What is there to be nervous about?"

Touch him, a voice whispered to me. Asmodeus itself, come to bear witness. But all the tenor of its voice had been stripped away, and with it, the heavy thrum of fear I often felt. Asmodeus' voice was a warm and welcoming thing, an embrace to urge me forward. *He wants to touch him, to slip inside. Give him everything you've ever wanted to give another man. Take from him your pleasure; be rough or gentle, but enjoy it. Make him enjoy you.*

I ran my hands over his chest, fingers grazing over his nipples. Vassago's smile was gentle but lustful. He settled back into the pillows and spread his legs, and the sight was delectable. I wanted to consume the feast of his flesh.

I pressed our cocks together and rutted forward. The both of us gasped as hundreds of pleasant jolts spread throughout our bodies. The friction was delicious, but not enough. I wanted more. Vassago reached up and held his legs apart. I dragged the leaking tip of my cock to his hole.

"*Please*," Vassago murmured, eyes dark with lust.

And I pushed it all in.

Vassago's hole opened for me with ease, and I sank all the way inside.

"Oh. *Oh*..."

"Fuck—ah!" Vassago cried, and a garbled noise escaped him when I slowly drew my cock out, focused on feeling the smooth walls and tight clench of the sphincter over the sensitive head. With only the tip remaining inside, I plunged back into the warmth with a heavy thrust.

Vassago wailed. His hands tightened around his calves, and his brows crashed together. His mouth hung open, and his spine arched.

He was wanton. Pathetic. *Beautiful*. My heart seized at the sight of him, another man exposing himself to me, opening his body for my pleasure.

All I could think of was the tight heat hugging my length, the walls convulsing as Vassago moaned and squeezed. I thrust in and out of him slowly, feeling every part of him; my whole body trembled with the pleasure.

How had I. *Managed*. For so long. Without *this?*

I knew if I fucked him how my body wanted, I would reach climax in moments. I relaxed the muscles in my lower belly in the hopes I could delay orgasm, and I grinded my hips down until *something* happened, and Vassago's hole relaxed so much I felt the warmth of his insides envelop part of my balls.

"That's it," I whispered, as the feeling changed. Now that Vassago was relaxed, I pounded into him without care. I was ruthless, thrusting hard and revelling in every reaction the demon had: his breathless gasps, heavy cries, Vassago's deep voice growing steadily higher in pitch with every thrust. Then Vassago's eyes snapped open, lust and fear and delight filling up his brown eyes, and each slick fuck had Vassago screaming.

Then, I slowed and moved slowly. Vassago's hands wrapped around my head. He pulled me down into a kiss and moaned into my mouth as we moved together, the divots of our pelvis locking together perfectly. He turned his head, and I dove into his neck, kissing and licking the exposed flesh there.

"You feel—so good," I told him.

Our chests were connected. Sweat pulled between us. I didn't care—I loved the noises I was pulling from this man. I loved the way he was looking at me, like I was a divine thing.

This slow pace only made the mounting pleasure difficult to ignore. He felt it, too; his hand was between his thighs, and he was rutting up eagerly into the palm of his hand. At one particularly deep thrust, Vassago's eyes slipped to the back of his skull, and I felt his hole clench.

"*There*," he breathed, and so I focused on the knot of nerves I had found, pressing into it again and again in time with Vassago's moans. "Yes," he cried out. "Yes, that feels *so*—"

Vassago came in a silent scream that melted into a long, protracted moan. His hole spasmed just as cum spurted from his cock. Vassago fell back, still in the throes of his climax, and I pounded into the wet heat with a desperation. My cock was pulsing, throbbing—I stared down at the moaning mess of a man beneath me and squeezed the two soft cheeks of his ass. I rammed up into him three more times, and seconds later, with Vassago's hole *clenching* tightly around me, I came hard inside him. I spilled everything I had into that man.

My own moan had me throwing my head back with pleasure. I kept moaning and thrusting, even when the sensation became unbearably sensitive. I wanted to milk myself of every last drop.

When the exhaustion hit, I closed my eyes and spent a moment suspended over Vassago's body.

Then I pulled out slowly, watching as his hole fought to keep my deflating cock inside. When I popped out, my cum oozed free in a gush. I moaned, thumbing the liquid back into Vassago's hole. He looked positively ravished. The sweat sheen on his forehead had made his hair stick to his skin. His eyes were heavy. Drool dripped from the corner of his mouth. And I loved what I had done to him: that I had filled him up like a prophetic dream, the way the fear of God had always filled me up. In fucking Vassago, I had made myself relaxed.

I slumped down beside him, and we moved close to hold one another—something I had never truly experienced. As the vulnerability bubbled up in me, I fought it down, thinking to myself that I was well beyond such worries now.

Instead, a new worry was filling me.

I longed for Asmodeus.

The realisation hit me like a curse. I *wanted* Asmodeus, all of it. I wanted it to treat me as I had treated Vassago; for it to look into my eyes and see my desire and my love. So, too, did I want its total domination. I wanted to be a mewling mess and lover; slave and taken care of.

Vassago looked more human than ever. He breathed heavily, air whistling through his nose as if he was asleep. But what was more terrifying than a demon who could make you forget he was one?

I turned and lay on my back, letting myself fantasise that this was my life: that I was still alive, as human as I had once been, and committed to a man like Vassago's bed rather than to the cloth. Would it have mattered, I wondered—for such a thing would not have been possible. The blasphemy, the constant threat of sin and being discovered, all would have destroyed me in some way or another.

Again, I thought: this was the only solution for me. Coming to Hell.

I closed my eyes and reached out for Asmodeus. Bravery filled me up. I told it, "I wish you and I will make love. I wish you would wreck me and leave me in the afterglow of rough pleasure. But so too do I wish you will love me."

I didn't know, in truth, what I wanted or what I was asking. Could I really assume a demon of Asmodeus' standing would ever have anything beyond lustful feelings for me? I had admitted to many demons along the way that I knew I was nothing special; just another set of holes for the demon to fuck.

But now I said, "Call me your little priest. Mean it when you say you are proud of me. These are things I wish for but not things I need."

Because in the end, I would take whatever it had to give me. Sex or soft touches, a rough breaking, or a slow loving—I would be Asmodeus' toy.

I slept by some miracle, and when bright morning sliced through the window against my eyelids, I snapped awake in terror. Scrambling up, the sheets gathered at my waist, and I cast about expecting all manner of things, all manner of evils. A part of me thought I was still a priest, just little Alessandro about to be chastised for sleeping in well past a respectable time. The rest of me thought: *why am I still in this bed?*

None of the other demons had done more than their duty with me, really. But when I turned, Vassago was staring up at me through those long lashes, and several emotions vied for my attention—fear, hope, lust, a strange despair. I must not have hidden any of it, for Vassago pushed up from the mattress and cooed to me, running a smooth hand across my face.

"There is no need for this," he whispered lovingly. A hot breath rolled off my neck as leaned forward, lips parting against my ear. "You are so close, little priest."

With all the eagerness of a child, I pressed my forehead against his face. Clutching at *something*—I needed the approval of this man, this *demon*, before I could extricate myself from his bed.

"A Duke," I whispered. "I please a Duke, and then I am before my Lord once more."

Vassago held my face and kissed me, not with any passion, but with a gentleness it felt odd for him to possess.

"The bibliotheca awaits you," he whispered, and took both of my hands. Naked, the two of us rose, and he walked me to the window of his tower. Beneath, many demons still gathered and called for his attention, but Vassago was looking out at the mountainous distance.

"Let us burn away the final dregs of shame. Let us fill you up with fiery love that goes beyond passion. You do not have to be confused for much longer: whatever is left to hold you back will be eliminated soon."

I said nothing as he leaned forward and pressed his lips against my eyelids. He led me away from the window to the far wall where he waved his hand. Bricks dispersed, colliding against one another in their desperation to move out of the way. As they folded into one another impossibly fast, I saw the design of beautiful coloured tiles poking out from beneath.

The design revealed itself to be quite human in appearance, the same as Vassago himself. Stretching green vines looped over bright yellow tile in a confronting hue. It reminded me of all the Italian hamlets I had visited. More bricks shifted, and I was staring at a fireplace, one absurdly large, with an opening tall enough to fit a person. If this fireplace had been functional, I imagined all the soot would smoke up Vassago's room in a few heartbeats.

"Step inside." Vassago gave a gentle but insistent push toward the open maw. A cast iron grate sat low, and I had to step over it, feet crunching against the husks of firewood that promptly fell to ash beneath the force of my weight.

Vassago smiled. He raised his fingers and his clicked fore-finger and thumb together. Fire erupted from the motion, engulfing his hand, and in the burn of the flame, I saw part of his true form revealed: long black fingernails curled over reddish skin, his hands elongated unnaturally. A thrill ran through me at his deception.

"Good luck," he whispered before setting me aflame.

The fire rushed from his fingers into the fireplace, and it wasn't the ashy wood that caught alight, but I.

I was consumed by heat. Flame burrowed into my skin; I felt it drying and cracking off, curling over and over into itself as it was eaten alive, exposing my tendons and the red flesh of my innards. I screamed. The pain was indescribable—sudden, all-consuming, inescapable. There was nothing but the fire. I was going to die. I was already dead. I thrashed and wailed in the fireplace, howling, and in my head, I was begging for it to end. Why had Vassago done this? Why had I trusted him?

But halfway through my next impassioned wail, the pain abruptly stopped.

I opened my eyes to find myself squatting in a fireplace with my body intact, like nothing at all had happened to it. I patted myself down, making sure, half expecting my skin to slough off in wide sheets.

Nothing.

I stood too fast on my way out of the fireplace, smacking my head against the arch and scattering ashes beyond the grate. Stumbling free, I skidded to a stop as I realised I was not in Vassago's domain any longer.

He had done what I had asked.

The Bibliotheca awaits, he'd said.

The fireplace had deposited me in a sleek, thin tower room. Bookshelves ran floor to ceiling with only the faintest slits between shelves to act as windows. Narrow rays of silvery light cleaved through the dark. A cast iron staircase lay to my right, and I took it, spiralling down from this top room to another and another until, finally, I came to a larger landing. It was there that I discovered the sigil for the Duke.

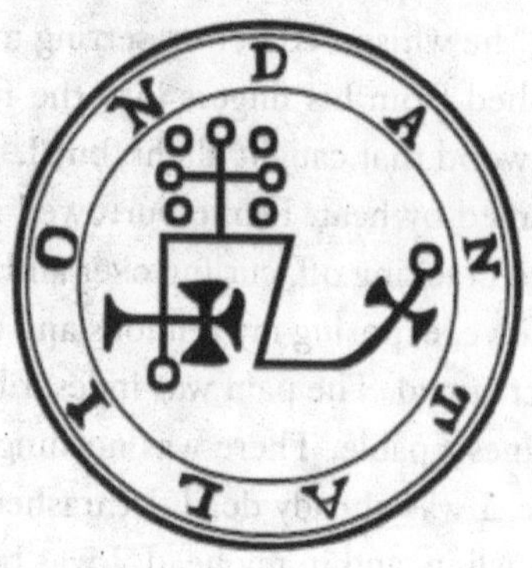

I WAS AT ONCE RELIEVED and terrified. I went before the sigil but made no quick moves to summon the demon. Instead, I pondered on what Vassago had taught me and what I had promised my Lord Asmodeus, and I—froze.

There was still a great fantasy of mine I hadn't much explored. So much of my life had involved the institution of my faith, and for too long, that had been a source of my fear.

If I wanted to be Asmodeus' completely, what would I have to do to be free of that?

Could I ever be free of those thoughts when it was my long-held lust, my shame at my longing, that led me to summon Asmodeus in the first place?

I closed my eyes and centred myself. For years, I had entrusted a God who had never answered my call. Asmodeus *had* answered. What was I doing by not trusting its ability?

Asmodeus had chosen all the demons I had encountered

for one reason or another: for my pleasure, for its pleasure, or to unburden me of the shackles in my mind.

Whoever this Duke was, I imagined the demon would know intrinsically how it was supposed to touch me. How it was supposed to change me.

There was no knife by the sigil, but as I looked around the landing—dense with paraphernalia for study and the like—I found a plain-handled dagger waiting for me. I slipped it out from beneath the books and did once more what I needed to do; I sliced deep to draw forth blood and offered it to the sigil.

Something compelled me to bow before the magic had even taken effect. I pressed my face into the aged hardwood, breathing in dust and mildew and age. A gurgling sounded as my blood was consumed, and the silvery light cast by the moon grew briefly stronger, sending large boxy highlights across the floor. I squeezed my eyes shut even tighter.

I could sense this demon almost in the way I could sense Asmodeus. The power of it loomed large in my mind, like something always in the corner of my eye: a shadow whose size was inescapable. Call it the nearness to my Lord, or simple wishful thinking: in any case, I knew when it had manifested before the floorboards creaked with the sudden new weight. Even with my eyes closed, I could feel it craning over me. Then footsteps shifted, the weight of the demon moving, and a chill went through me—not heat the way I felt beneath Asmodeus' touch.

A long, clawed hand reached into my hair. I melted beneath the touch, catlike with my eagerness, pushing into the touch like it might save me from what came next.

It didn't, of course.

The hand tightened, sweet grip becoming rough, and suddenly I was being wrenched to my feet by a fistful of my hair.

I yelped, pain searing in my follicles and then in sharp jolts down my neck and back. I scrabbled in the air, squirming, eyes closed against the pain.

"Look upon me," a voice commanded.

It was husky, a deep whisper. Compelled to obey, I opened my eyes. For a while, I could see nothing but the umbral pool of its gaze. No other features made themselves known to me.

"What is thy name?" the voice asked.

"Alessandro," I told it. "I am Asmodeus'—"

"Toy in training," it breathed. "I am aware."

A second passed and it was only the two of us breathing. I smelled of sweat; I was sure I smelled of sex. This demon smelled of pine and ocean breeze.

"And you?" I whispered. I shook slightly in its grasp. "What name do you keep, lord?"

It exhaled nosily and lowered me to the ground. All the while, I could only see its unblinking gaze.

"Dantalion," it told me. "Duke of Hell."

Like that, my pin-hole vision was revoked, and the whole room's vision came hurtling back.

The Duke was very tall. It wore a long, great robe that, from the right angle, I could have mistaken for a cassock. Its visage slipped into the uncanny, bearing both the faces of men and women and oscillating between them with each blink of its two eyes. Even *they* rapidly changed in size, shape, and colour. What was fascinating to me appeared ever banal for the demon: this was simply how it looked, like everybody and nobody at once.

"If you know who I am, then you know my plight and what I must accomplish here."

Perhaps my eagerness was getting the best of me: I wanted nothing more than to be used and sent to Asmodeus. I had forgotten everything I had promised Asmodeus and, frankly, could not be bothered spending time on overcoming whatever human traumas were keeping me in my shame.

How fickle of me. How brash. I had clearly learned nothing.

Dantalion looked down at me, eyes shifting in size and shape but never in emotion: always, its eyes showed the faintest hint of disdain. Of pity. I shrunk beneath it. "I do not wish to have thee," it said.

"Then we are at an impasse, my Duke," I said whilst shaking, my whole body contorting on the ground. "For I must fulfil my Lord's wishes, and as its underling, you must do the same."

Where had this brashness come from, if not from my wilful and desperate desire? Dantalion looked at me and said nothing, but the pity in the inky wells of its eyes made me shudder. With almost petulant silence, Dantalion turned its back on me and began to pace its own library, finger gliding over tomes. It selected one and moved to the corner, where it draped itself like a beautiful, terrifying ornament.

I stared.

Dantalion had an age to it, an ancient thing, and yet, in this moment, the demon felt adolescent.

"What is it you are usually summoned for?"

Dantalion gave an affronted huff. "He draws blood for me without even knowing what he wants, and what I have to offer." The demon glanced up slightly from its reading. "An apt descriptor of thee, I presume?"

I flushed because it was entirely correct. I knew what I wanted in vague terms. I was frightened to demand my own pleasure. I had told Asmodeus I would overcome this by the time I returned to its side, but I couldn't fight the cotton-mouthed feeling in me to tell Dantalion.

The demon's eyes narrowed. I expected it to push me as so many other demons had. Even Furcus had, in the end, wanted to plough me, to root his seed in me—despite the hours of talk beforehand. Dantalion—I couldn't be sure it even wished to look upon me.

With nothing to do, I stood and gazed upon the library Dantalion kept. The Bibliotheca. Since the demon hadn't evaporated, I assumed it would stay summoned until we fulfilled our joining. This gave me ample time to explore.

I thumbed a tome made of white leather, pricked with a soft down, like feathers. The first few lines read;

ON HEAVEN'S Hierarchy of Angels
Penned by the Seventh Angelic Scribe

THE SOUND of a book being roughly slammed, and then brisk, sudden air—the sense of *mass* behind me, boxing me in between bookshelf and body. Clawed fingers rose over shoulder and plucked the tome from my grasp.

"Not for your eyes."

I spun to Dantalion. "That was a book from Heaven."

"I am a demon. Why does thievery surprise you?"

I glanced at other tomes, which looked nothing like the books I had seen in Furcus' realm. So many of those had been empty save for the knowledge I craved. I said, "Furcus had—"

A scoff. "All the books in that Knight's sad excuse for a library comes from mine."

"What were you, in Heaven?"

Dantalion turned to me, grip flexing over the spine of the tome again and again. "What I am here."

"Which is?"

"Startling bored. Keeper of old tomes. Cowed by the whims of humans. I—"

"I need your help."

I said it suddenly and felt much smaller and younger than my thirty-five years. Dantalion must have seen it in me, that kernel of weakness or of innocence to be crushed, for it came closer to me, fingers flexing as if it were about to point.

"There," it said. "Have courage. You have already summoned me; your heart has a desire. Speak it."

Was its new eagerness genuine? Was this glee because in speaking, I would leave its domain sooner? I eyed Dantalion and turned bodily toward it, pressing close.

Rage flashed in Dantalion's eyes. When I reached up to touch its face, it slammed its fingers around my wrist, holding me still.

It bared its teeth, showed me how strange and sharp they were, but as it regarded me, the anger died away.

"You mean to anger me," it said, "to avoid speaking your desire."

I went limp against it. I was a man and yet a child in this sense. I turned away. My chest seized with guilt, with shame —*why?* After all this time, after whoring myself and enjoying it, after making love to Vassago, *why* did it panic me so to say what I wanted?

"Tell me what you would do to me first," I whispered.

Dantalion hissed. "A way for you to cheat, a dilution of your desire, if you can spot your own inside mine."

I looked up at it. Tears stung my eyes—ridiculous! My response made no sense. I enjoyed my desire. I partook in sexual acts. Was it really so difficult to open my mouth and say, *I want this, and this, and this?*

"I want. . .to know what I want."

Dantalion let go of my wrist and pressed a finger to my lips. "You know what you want. You proved that with the Prince Vassago. You are just afraid of your wants."

That was true enough. If I closed my eyes, I could recall living as I had. More than two decades of a lust-filled haze could only be survived through repression. Through self-denial. It had been the bravest thing, to throw it all off and choose Asmodeus. But in choosing Hell and this path, I had still been answering the call of another: of Asmodeus itself.

What would it look like if I'd answered my own call? What would my life have looked like if I had given in long ago?

Oliviero came to me unbidden. My fantasy, realised through the apparition of him on his knees, tongue on me, lips sucking over my rosary. If I had faced him in reality and told him my carnal desires, he would have been appalled.

They all would have. Wouldn't they?

I said none of this, but when I looked up at Dantalion, its eyes were bright and hungry.

"Do you wish to find out?" it whispered.

A gasp escaped my lips. "Another fantasy?" I whispered. "I —I could want that. I *do* want that. I would want to enter Oliviero. I want—"

"If it were not a fantasy, what then?"

I didn't understand. I frowned at the demon and gestured to the grand structure of its bibliotheca. "I am dead, my Duke. I committed a mortal sin to enter here. I am no human any longer."

And Dantalion smiled, faces and lips oscillating in shape and size and colour. "This is something I can give you. This is what I, Duke of Hell, can do. A small amount of time, anywhere in the mortal realm. When the time is up, you *will* return: there is no way for you to survive longer than my allowance. Your spirit will return here, to the bibliotheca, to me. But if you have unfinished business, as it appears you do, then how will you be my Lord's plaything wholeheartedly?"

I swallowed and gestured at it. "You cannot pretend you have no interest in me, if you are willing to do this."

Dantalion conceded with a shrug. "I have an interest."

"It is my duty to bring you pleasure. If I don't—"

"What I want to do is akin to torture for you," Dantalion snapped quickly. "Perhaps in your mind, there is still denial at what your brethren think of you. You think: *perhaps they never rolled the rocks away. Perhaps they never found the bishop and mine corpses. My death might be a holy tragedy to them*. But the real holy tragedy is your true nature, and if you go to them now, they will know with certainty exactly what creature you are. What kind of man they supped with all those years. I am curious to see if you will follow through."

But Dantalion's words had stirred me. Rather literally—the thrill of the transgression filled my body with untampered heat. I wanted that.

I wanted them to see me. I wanted them all to know. I desired both the humiliation and the ultimate freedom of their knowledge: I would never be able to hide again.

I would never return, not ever, to anything other than this.

So I met Dantalion's eye with defiance.

"I want that," I told it. "I want them to know exactly what kind of man I am."

$$\maltese \quad 8 \quad \maltese$$

The abbey smelled as I remembered it: altar candles, amber, frankincense, the aged books, and the sweet summer air of Italy. A cloying and inescapable mix. I used to think I was breathing in God with every breath.

It happened like this: Dantalion spoke in some infernal language I could never hope to understand, and when I next opened my eyes, I was standing in the nude in one of the abbey's many halls.

To return was jarring. I'd been deposited in a thankfully empty hallway. The windows to my right, a simple paned glass, showed me it was night time—a swathe of black shadow hid everything. I could see nothing much inside, either: no candles were lit in the wall sconces this evening. It was past the time that many priests entered their silent hours, where they wouldn't speak again until morn.

I didn't know what I was doing, but I felt anxious. Not frightened, but certainly surprised at myself for going through with this. In a way, it all felt like a dream—the consequences I would face would always end in my inevitable return to Hell. But I would still have to face the look of disgust on my brethren's faces.

When I oriented myself, I decided first to visit Oliviero's room. This involved feeling along the walls and letting my eyes adjust, though I found I had much better sight in the dark than I had when I was alive. When I found his door, I rapped my knuckles softly against the wood and waited tensely to be admitted.

My knocking was not answered.

Reluctantly, I pulled away from the door and began to walk towards the main chapel. My feet touched the cold stone. Breathing felt difficult, like I hadn't truly done it in months.

How long had I been gone?

Unabashed at my nakedness, I continued toward the chapel. I turned corners, and slowly but surely, more light began to filter in as dozens of candles had been lit and seemed to guide me onwards.

It took little for me to recognise this layout. I had been wrong in my initial assessment: the silence was not because many monks and priests were in silent hours but because all of them were attending a vigil.

"Quod autem vobis dico omnibus dico vigilate." Secundum S. Marcum

"What I say to you, I say to all: keep watch." Gospel according to St. Mark

Vigils—a period of watchfulness, a night spent in prayer, community, and reflection. I pressed my body to the cold stone wall and peered around the bend, where the doors to the chapel were shut. Candles dotted the floor and cast a sunset glow over the double doors. From within, I could hear the murmurings of communal prayer; the voice of a single man and the occasional answer from his gathered flock.

I understood what Dantalion meant by torture. This was not as simple as a confession to one man. This was humiliation drawn out. *All* of them would know me for what I was. *All* of them.

A swarm of negative emotions swamped me, and I threw myself back against the stone, pressing close and breathing as slowly as I could manage. My breathing came shallowly, and I pressed my hands against my ribs, feeling the flare of the bone as it dug into my palm.

I closed my eyes. All I had to do was turn the corner and wrench open the doors. I would find Oliviero and confess my desires, and he would shun me, as they all would. I would at least be free of the shackles of my shame: I would be true to my nature.

In my head, I heard the rumbling of Lord Asmodeus' voice.

My little lamb of a priest. Know that I am here with you, always. What do you fear from their judgement?

I opened my eyes, and my breathing slowed. "I fear the judgement itself, not the effect. God cannot touch me now. But my shame can. It has its hand around my throat."

Replace that hand with mine. Let me squeeze the life from your shame. Prove to me you know yourself and show these priests what kind of man they worshipped with for decades.

I took a deep, centring breath and propelled myself around the corridor, barrelling toward the closed doors with ferocity. Against the wood, I splayed both my hands and felt nothing from the wood: no force of magic, none of God's presence, nothing but the threat of a splinter against my fingers.

I pushed.

The doors gave way with a deep whine. They opened onto a stage of candles and holy light. I saw at the altar at the end of the aisle and before it the abbot, head bowed, murmuring a prayer. The pews were filled with novices, monks, and ordained priests joining him. My arrival sparked no interest—I could have been a priest late to the vigil; they did not even glance up—and so I closed the doors and slunk to the side behind one of the pillars to spy upon my cohort a little longer.

The doors opened again suddenly, and in filed two novices carrying a large vessel between them. Towels of cream linen were draped over their shoulders.

As they moved up the aisle, the abbot stood to greet them. It was then I saw he was—new.

Not the abbot who had served when I was here, though, without a doubt, I had visited this chapel many times. Again, the fear rose in me that I had been out of time and that the Earth had continued to spin without my presence. How long had it been?

Who was that man?

"Thank you, brothers," he said, voice as sweet as the scent of a rose. The two novices deposited the vessel in front of him, heads bowed in reverence. "You may sit." They dashed into the pews without another word, and my gaze fell on the vessel.

It was made of a lightly beaten bronze, and I recognised it as something used in a certain ritual: the Mandatum, a central part in the Holy Thursday celebration.

Jesus had washed the feet of his disciples. The abbot was about to do the same.

Around me, my brothers began to sing the *Ubi Caritas*:

UBI CARITAS ET AMOR, Deus ibi est.

Congregavit nos in unum Christi amor.
Exsultemus, et in ipso jucundemur.

WHERE CHARITY AND LOVE ARE, *God is there.*
Love of Christ has gathered us into one.
Let us rejoice in Him and be glad.

I WATCHED as one from the crowd shifted. He wore not the usual clerical cassock but a much simpler garb. His feet were bare. He approached the altar and bowed to it first before he nodded to the abbot, who let him approach.

And the abbot went down onto his knees.

When the abbot looked up, hair shifting from his face and candlelight finally making his appearance known, I gasped.

I recognised him. Beautiful blond curls, grown in a soft crown around his head. Those kind eyes, those sweet lips.

It was Oliviero! Only, *older.*

How long had I been gone?

I watched with rapt attention as Oliviero reached out and cupped the proffered foot of the priest. He took one of the linen towels, dipped it in the water, and brought it against the man's foot.

The holy sound of singing did nothing to dampen the eroticism of the moment. Even in supplication, or perhaps *especially* in supplication, Oliviero looked divine and beautiful. My stomach lurched watching him drag the wet cloth up and down the man's leg. I watched the priest as he tensed his calf, as the hair around his ankle became sodden, as he was forced to lean on Oliviero's shoulder for balance. I stayed watching for nearly an hour as man after man stood and offered his foot, and Oliviero took them with kindness and washed them the way Jesus washed the feet of his disciples the day before his death. And guilt rose in me, because I could look upon this and understand its significance for the men gathered here, but I could tell I was not among them in any proper way. My nature was not this: I could never have participated in this innocently. I never had. Even when the abbot washed my feet and made me shiver with fear, I would watch the way my brothers peeled away their robs from their calves. I focused on the curl of dark hair against warm skin; I thought about my mouth as the cloth, just as wet and just as thorough as it kissed those men's feet.

When there was no further movement from the seated brothers, I took what little courage I had and made myself step out from hiding. I walked down the aisle, eyes fixed on Oliviero. As I moved, murmurs rose around me. My naked form had caused a stir. And some of my brothers must still be here, for I heard:

"*Alessandro?*"

"*Is that Don Alessandro?*"

"*O, our Lord God!*"

I ignored them all. My eyes were fixed on Oliviero, head down in quiet prayer. When the aisle carpet ended, the sound of my bare feet slapped against the stone, and he was pulled from his contemplation by that and the sound of his congregation.

He recognised me instantly. I saw it in his eyes, a flare of surprise and hope and fear. His mouth parted softly. I saw him as the boy he had been, the beautiful young man so full of innocence. His hands, which were clasped in front of his face, let go of one another and gripped the air as he stumbled to his feet. He reached for both my hands.

"Alessandro?"

I didn't reply right away. His recognition of me sent the gathered priests into tense silence. The creaking of pews filled the chapel as bodies shifted, leaning forward with intense interest.

Oliviero clasped my hands. He stood half bent, as if contemplating genuflection. "I never believed—the accusations. Has God returned you to us? Does He wish us to know the truth? Forgive us, we—"

"Oliviero," I whispered, "How long has it been?"

"Ten years," he said without question. "I am nearly the age you were when you left us." His gaze went past me to where some of the brethren had risen from their places. A few were on their knees in more fervent prayer. "This is no vision? You can see him too?"

I cupped Oliviero's face and returned his attention to me. "I must speak with you."

"Of course. Of *course*—but I—the bishop must know. This is—a holy miracle! I—"

"It is not," I said.

I watched Oliviero's face fall. I had to be truthful with him in order to be truthful to myself. Still touching Oliviero's face, I turned to my gathered brethren, many of which I recognised and many I did not. I told them, "I must tell you what has happened to me and how it came about. I must do this for my own conscience, and for my future."

And, of course, they all agreed. That was how faith worked.

Before I spoke, I asked Oliviero to divulge what had happened to my body.

He shook his head. "We never managed to clear the entrance to the cave," he said, quite solemnly. "Both you and Bishop Fazio could not have your bodies buried properly. There were rumours. Accusations of foul play. But please know, we did everything we could, and we prayed for your immortal soul."

Prayers that went to waste.

It was as Dantalion had suggested. They knew nothing. It *was* a particular torture, knowing I would be solely responsible for destroying the image they had of me.

"We must tell the bishop!" someone called from the crowd.

"Find him a cassock. Food—we must—"

They meant well. They were still fuelled by a peculiar kind of innocence I had never possessed.

I looked Oliviero in the eye, passed my thumb across his lip, and said, "I was in Hell."

I said it just quietly enough for Oliviero to hear. I expected—outrage. Some cry of panic. Instead, he looked me in the eye, pursed his lips, and went down onto his knees.

He was so close to me that his breath warmed all parts of my body on the way down. My hands fell away from his face, and I watched him curiously as he took his damp cloth and began to clean my feet. It was as if he couldn't—or wouldn't—believe what I had said.

"God returned you to us," he whispered, conspiratorial; he didn't want the others to hear.

"A demon returned me," I said—louder. The novices in the front row bristled. I watched one rise from his seat in a panic.

"Alessandro," Oliviero chided. Still, he washed, eyes downcast. Age had not made him any less beautiful.

"Kiss my foot," I whispered.

He froze. The praying had stopped, and so too had the cries for my return. The only sound in the abbey was the faint flutter of flame and of men breathing. In and out. In and out. Oliviero finally began to look up through his long lashes. A flush had bloomed upon his cheeks.

I do not know why he obeyed me, but ever so slowly, Oliviero leaned down without breaking eye contact and pressed his lips to my raised foot. His grip tightened around my ankle. I wobbled, forced to clutch his shoulder for support. The movement of my groin caught his eye, just briefly.

"Did you not hear me?" I asked him.

"I heard you."

"Then?"

"Why would God have sent you to Hell? You were kind, Alessandro. You were a good man. You stand before me now —a *good* man."

Guilt swarmed me. It hurt to destroy this image, but I needed him to know the truth.

I wanted him to know whose foot he had just kissed.

I pressed forward with my foot, grazing his freshly shaven chin. His mouth opened in surprise. I could have pressed my foot inside his mouth if I had wished, made him suck, defiled both him and this ritual all at once.

"I sent myself there," I told him. "I whored myself to a demon. I made a covenant. Oliviero, can't you see? I want to free you all from your shame, a chain whose cuffs bite your skin for all your lives. You can be free of them."

The chapel's blissful quiet shattered. *"Blasphemy!"* someone called at the back.

"The bishop! We need to—"

"No demon may enter this holy place!"

"It is not Alessandro! A demon wears his—"

And throughout all the chaos, Oliviero still gripped my foot.

He looked up into my eyes and didn't pull away even as the commotion increased. The doors were thrown open, and some of the novices and priests fled. It could have been deathly silent or an orchestra of screams, and I would have heard nothing but the uneven breathing of the beautiful man before me.

He surprised me by speaking first. A furrow in his brow,

something in his eye. Fear had gripped his heart, but the way he clutched to me suggested he did not find me terrible.

Lowly, he said, "I dreamt of you, once. I dreamt you had me on my knees."

In my memory, I had said, "Open," and he had obeyed. In this second chance, I reached out, and he moved forward so slowly that I doubted he was even conscious of his movement.

Tears pricked in Oliviero's eyes. "I desired you carnally. You defiled my mouth."

"You wanted it," I whispered, a low growl forming in my throat. "You *begged* for it."

Oliviero's eyebrows crashed together, and I thought: Had that been a dream? I thought it had been a fantasy of my own design. But what if I had slipped into Oliviero's filthy concoction?

What if he really was like *me?*

Suddenly, Oliviero stood. Blood had made his cheeks a vibrant red, but he managed to appear calm. He clapped his hands together, and the sound echoed throughout the chapel, calming the storm of panicked voices instantly.

"Calm, brethren," he said. "I can deal with this. This demon has not come for any of you; it is a test for me. Don Alessandro was my fear friend and mentor. Calmly exit the chapel and close the doors. Go into private prayer—pray for the rest of the night! Whatever sounds you hear, do not open the doors to this chapel until I emerge. I will contact the bishop in the morning when I am victorious. Go, now. Quickly!"

His words encouraged a few pleas for his safety, but all of them fled. If everyone thought me a demon, so be it: I had told them all my true nature.

In the end, it had always been Oliviero who I wanted to know me.

It had always been Oliviero I had desired to corrupt.

When the doors finally closed, I watched him carefully. He stayed staring at those doors with his hands clasped. I could hear his breathing and smell the sweat that had started forming on his body. He glanced over his shoulder at me with a sudden gasp as if surprised I was still there.

"How," I whispered, "do you intend to deal with me?"

He said nothing. Fear had made him suddenly small. Oliviero squeezed his hands together, pressed his lips into a thin line, and regarded me with unbridled terror—and something else. Something more.

I moved behind him. He let me approach, stiffened only slightly when I wrapped my arms around his torso. I could only feel him slightly beneath the layers of the cassock. For a moment, I just held him.

I had loved Oliviero, hadn't I?

I held him for so long that I barely registered my own tears streaming down onto his neck.

"Alessandro?"

"I—missed you," I whispered.

He spun around, tearing out of my grasp and clutching my face. He made me look at him and crashed our foreheads together.

"Do not cry. Whatever you say—I remember you. I remember who you were. And to me, even if my youth frustrated you or my innocence irked you, you looked upon me with a kindness."

"I looked upon you with a lust," I said. "I'm sorry, and yet, I am not sorry. You are beautiful. You are still so beautiful. I've always wanted. . ."

He pulled me close into an embrace and shushed me. His body shook. He smelled of life and incense. I breathed in the scent caught in the divot of his neck. My hands roamed over the thick robe, ghosting over his groin, where I felt only the faintest outline of a bulge, my fingertips trailing over his upper thigh.

Now, it was my breath warming his skin, the only exposed patch of it rising above the white collar of his priestly cassock, and I felt alive again.

Perhaps I hadn't realised until that moment how badly I had wanted this. I had given in to some of my nature and not all of it: I wanted to take, I wanted to be used. I wanted affection. I wanted to meet another man in the same field of cautious yet overpowering attraction. Oliviero's breaths came in hot and fast.

"I cannot—" he murmured. "I serve God."

"God serves only Himself," I said. "You are my own age, now. I know that you feel it. The disappointment. The dying hope of being His chosen. You are becoming jaded, Oliviero —you *know* as well as I did that you have spent your life in service to an institution that does not value you, worshipping a God who either does not care that you exist or is so wholly cruel with his creations that He does not deserve our praise."

"Bl—blasphemy. . ."

"Oh, yes." I licked his ear, sucking on his lobe, dragging my tongue down his neck. "As blasphemous as one can get."

I pulled away from him to see his face, which was as red as the blood of Christ. I reached out, and he took my hand cautiously, letting me guide him up towards the altar.

We stared at it for a while. He turned to me, eyes wide.

"Why have you come?"

I took my time to answer. "I thought I had come to be rid of my shame," I began. I reached out for his hand. He squeezed it. I thought of Paul in that town, and Romans 10. Of brethren loving each other in a different way to how I loved men. I made sure to meet his eyes when I told Oliviero the truth.

"I have lusted for you since you arrived at the abbey. I

fantasised about you often. Perhaps more than that. Perhaps I. . .I believe I began to care for you. I wanted to corrupt you, and I wanted to love you the way men love women. That is my sin. That is what I gave up God for: Love of men."

Is it such a great sin? I wanted to ask him, but I fought the urge to scrounge around for his approval. Then I cupped his face and gently brought our lips together.

He gasped, breath-stopping as our lips touched. His eyes stayed open, staring into my very soul. He pulled away first, saying, "Like Judas."

And maybe it was like Judas; a kiss to betray the Lord God.

$\text{❧} \ 9 \ \text{❧}$

So I kissed him again, drawing his body close against mine. I pressed my tongue against his lips and felt a thrill when he let out the faintest of moans.

"I am ashamed," he admitted when I pulled away. "That dream haunted me. I thought of it again and again; went to confession for it again and again."

"You looked so beautiful like that," I told him, and his eyes went wide with the understanding that I had been there. That perhaps it hadn't been a dream at all.

"I still believe in God," he told me.

"I am not here to talk about love. I am here to talk about *us*. Do you feel what I feel?"

He did not answer me, turning away in shame. I reached out and pulled his chin back towards me.

"Tell me," I urged him. My eyes flickered down to where the bulge beneath his robes was growing steadily in size.

"*Yes*."

I crowded against him, turning his body so we were facing the altar. Then I pushed him up the steps until we were before the pure marble slab, lined with a purple cloth and covered with candles and crosses.

I made sure to disturb none of it as I pressed Oliviero face down onto the mensa. Then I carefully rolled up his cassock until it was bunched around his neck, and his whole lower half lay exposed to me.

His legs quivered. His feet were as bare as our brethren's, and I watched with desire as he strained on the tips of his toes, calf muscle bulging with the effort. He wore simple black shorts and a white linen shirt. I reached up, fingers gliding beneath the shirt to touch the belt of skin around his waist.

He shivered. "Wait—"

I stopped moving but kept my fingers pressed to him. "No one has to know."

"God will know," he whispered.

"God does not care half as much as you think it or wish it. I called to him for my whole life. Only Asmodeus answered."

"As is the devil's way." He was shivering, straining to look at me over his shoulder. But I wasn't holding him down anymore. He could have stood and run at any time.

He was just like me.

"I am no devil, nor demon. I'm a man, same as you. And I have wanted you for years."

He melted visibly, exhaling so shakily that he spread himself further across the mensa. One of the crosses wobbled precariously from a tap of his outstretched arms.

"If you participate and realise you were wrong—that you *hated* it, and you are full of shame—then repent and tell the truth to the bishop. Tell him a demon of lust took the form of Don Alessandro and, to save your brethren, you gave your-self to ensure their purity."

Oliviero quivered, "A lie."

"Is it?" I ran my hands up his exposed legs and tugged gently at the shorts. "Are you telling me you *do* want this?"

Oliviero gasped, evidently surprised at what he had said—at what he had realised about himself.

"I. . ." he whimpered. His body shifted away from my touch, though at times it would betray him, pressing back into me. His back was arched.

"Let me show you what I tore open Hell for," I breathed against his skin.

Barely a second passed before I heard him relax. He shivered and turned his face away from me. I knew the urge to hide one's face and I awarded him that vulnerability. He was regarding the cross, I thought. He was saying his own prayer.

But in the end, he could not resist.

"Yes." Mouse-like, ever so quiet. "Yes."

I gently pulled down his shorts.

Oliviero roughly inhaled, gasping as the chill touched his exposed ass. His skin was smooth, the hair fine in both colour and thickness. I gripped him, squeezing against the firm muscle. How good he looked stretched out like that. The swell of his balls hung beautifully between his legs. I pressed firmly against his lower back, encouraging him to spread further, and I caught a glimpse of his quivering hole.

I leaned into the crack between those two muscles and licked.

"*Ah!*"

Oliviero bucked in surprise, clenching hard. I pressed his cheeks apart, spreading them for better access. My gaze trickled down the length of Oliviero's spine. I thought I was well past the days of considering myself a holy man, but I understood something in the alabaster perfection of his body; how easy it could be to worship.

I buried my face right in the middle of him, slowly, as if not to spook an animal. I nuzzled, opening my breath to exhale warm breath. It was enough to make Oliviero pigeon-toed, knees turning inward as he fought himself. He bowed his head, and I heard a soft, near-impatient whine. Vassago had made me love this, and how I wanted to see Oliviero melt with pleasure. I grazed my stubble against him, and he bucked toward me. His balls lurched upwards, and I pressed the broad, flat span of my tongue to his hole. Oliviero's cry was ragged. I dragged my tongue over him in long laps, and then in circling motions, teasing at the knotted muscle as it pulsed and squeezed. The sound grew increasingly sloppy; there was the wetness, my rough breathing, and Oliviero's whines. But I could draw more out of him: I wanted to hear him beg, to moan my name, to become so wanton and free that he was transformed by his pleasure. I pressed the tip of my tongue to him and pushed, pushed, *pushed* inside. Splayed as he was, I was the one who bounced back and forth, neck bobbing to fuck forward with my tongue. Every thrust made Oliviero squirm, his knees turning inward.

"Good boy," I told him when I next stopped for air. "You're being so good for me."

"I—" Oliviero started, but embarrassment overcame him. He buried his head into the crook of his elbow and tried to muffle his moans. With my tongue free, I pressed my left thumb into his hole, using the rest of my left hand to grab his ass. With my right, I reached up to his stiff cock, perilously hard. I drew his hips away from the altar so there was room, and I squeezed my hand around his length. Thumb moving, I matched the rhythm to my strokes. Oliviero bucked and strained and moaned, and my mouth welled with drool at the sight of his desperation.

He came fast, splattering the concave curl of his chest, and he collapsed with sudden shame, whimpering on the altar.

I stood and leaned over him, needing to give my own cock a quick, nearly unconscious squeeze to stay me.

I could put him on his knees and use the wet channel of his throat, as I had in Hell, but I wanted more. I wanted to gape him, to make him understand the pleasure of being filled; of being made complete.

"You became an abbot. You dedicated your life to this. But you feel it, don't you? What I felt?" I rested on his body, moving the mess of blond curls away from his forehead. I kissed his cheek, rubbing my lips against the sweat-coated skin. "Let me inside you. Let me *fuck* you, Oliviero."

He let out a low, long buried moan. His body shivered; he was vulnerable post-orgasm, logic stripped away.

"Mhm," he said, but I need more than that.

"Tell me what you want," I say.

"No, I. . ." A panicked edge overcame his voice. He half pushed away, gathering the cloth laid over the altar in his fist. "I can't. I can't."

"I need you to."

I said nothing more, but I stepped forward and rubbed my hips against his ass, slipping my cock between the crack and resting the tip against the saliva-coated hole.

"Oh, hh. . ." Oliviero gasped. He made an abortive roll of his hips before he panicked and looked away.

I wanted to see Oliviero's face. "Turn over for me."

He obliged almost instantly. I watched with rapt attention as he lowered himself to the flat of his feet and, melting, rolled onto his back at an uncomfortable arch. He looked— pathetic. Beautiful. Gorgeous and wanting. He looked just as I had imagined him all those years ago. The cassock had gathered excessively around his chest, making his body appear exceptionally small as it emerged from the fabric.

If you're going to be my bitch, you won't be wearing God's dog collar.

Asmodeus had said that to me and forced me to remove it. But I was different.

I liked to know that God was watching.

But I wanted to see more of Oliviero.

Carefully, I raised my fingers to the rounded fabric buttons closing his cassock and undid them one by one. The collar I slipped out with two fingers, and I put the cotton against Oliviero's lips. "Open."

He opened, and I pushed in. He bit down hard on the fabric with a whine.

Slowly, I opened the cassock up and tugged him free of it, discarding the garment on the floor by my feet.

He scrambled back onto the mensa, knocking over several crosses. He looked around with uncomprehending horror, fingers shaking as he reached to right them. I stepped forward and pressed my cock against his belly.

Oliviero stopped moving, eyes wide as he regarded me.

"Tell me what you want," I asked again, reaching down to pluck the collar from his teeth.

He looked up at me with sudden defiance. "I don't know. I'm scared. I want—" he said nothing, only paused. "But I—I do not wish God to see."

"Let him see."

I ran my hands up his thighs and around his slowly hardening member. His eyes stared at my cock, painfully hard against him. He reached for it haltingly.

I encouraged him with, "I want you to touch me."

He exhaled loudly and rolled his palm around it. "Oh, *Lord.*"

I watched as his cock jumped to sudden life.

I worked him slowly, and he worked me, eyes fixated on my cock and the way the foreskin bunched and stretched over the swollen glands. His eyes filled with surprise, with tears, with pleasure.

I reached past him to the anointing oil sitting on the altar. "Watch me," I commanded him, though he was the most attentive audience I'd ever had. I dipped my forefinger and middle finger inside and drew them out, coated and glistening. My thumb rubbed up and down my fingers, ensuring every inch of skin was slick with it.

"Tell me."

"I—" Oliviero blushed further. He couldn't look in my eyes. "I want it."

With my other hand, I roughly snatched his chin. He hissed, pained, and I shook firmly until I was certain he wasn't looking away. "*Tell* me what you want."

Oliviero's lip buckled. The oil slick ran down my fingers and over my third knuckle. He panted, opened his mouth, closed it, his skin blistering red with his shame. "I want you."

"*Oliviero!*" I bellowed, frustrated.

He squeezed his eyes shut. "I want you inside me! I want you to fuck me! I wish I had never become a novitiate; I wish I had lived as other men do! I am full of regret, and if you could just—show me! *Show* me what my body is meant to feel like!"

I drew him into a kiss so long and passionate I could feel the tears on his cheeks as they fell. Shame did that to you. Release did much the same.

"*I loved you,*" he whispered, brows crashing together as he stared up at me.

"I loved you, too," I said honestly, and I wiped away the tears from his cheek. "Are you ready?"

"I want it," he nodded, mouth open. "Put your fingers inside me."

I couldn't stop myself after that. My body convulsed, and my jaw went slack with submission. I brought my coated fingers to his hole, slotting them in the slightly widened indentation, pushing through any resistance until those two fingers slipped inside.

Oliviero was so aroused my fingers slipped in up to the second knuckle on entry. He moaned, clenching so tightly around them. His mouth hung wide open, jaw slack—completely unguarded. Completely vulnerable. I dropped my grip from his chin and wrapped my hand around his cock, squeezing just once. The motion made him unwind. He slumped against the altar, legs in the air, and I could pulse my fingers in and out of him with ease.

"Relax. Let me take care of you."

"Yes. Yes." He somehow flushed another shade darker as he said it, hands flying over his face, covering his eyes and his shame.

"Look at me," I breathed, pushing another finger inside him.

He convulsed, bucking up, and his hands flew away from his face with the shock of the feeling. I nearly took him then and there—my cock seized at the sight of him and his beauty.

Oliviero met my gaze.

I bucked forward, pressing my erection to the underside of his balls. Something changed in his body and his expression, a shift that moved him away from shame towards desire. I knew it intimately; I'd experienced it myself.

But I wanted to give Oliviero something I hadn't received that first time. I leaned over him and cupped his beautiful face in my hands. Our bodies pressed against one another. He shivered as if cold. I pressed my lips to his, waiting for his shivering to stop, and then I kissed him deeply, opening my mouth against the warmth of his lips. His legs fell open, and I collapsed on him, drawing myself ever closer as he wrapped his arms around my neck. Between our flush forms, I reached, drawing our cocks together between my fingers until they were pressed from root to tip. I rocked my hips against him, gripping the two of us in my right hand, all the while still kissing him. I pressed my tongue against his teeth, and he opened his lips with a moan. Bit by bit, his body understood what to do, and it wasn't so much about him relaxing anymore as it was about this bodily instinct; an innate understanding. An intrinsic want. He was like me, so well versed with fantasy and years of longing that, at the moment of reception, he *knew* what to do.

"*I want it*," he breathed against my lips.

"Be specific," I bade him, thumb gliding over his lower lip as if to coax the words from his mouth.

"*You*," he whispered, all reverent with his tone. Just as I had been with Asmodeus. "*Enter me. Defile me.*" Then, louder. "I don't care anymore. I want—"

He wanted, and that was what mattered. I wanted. The pair of us, who had been moulded by the church, flogged and scolded and bent into a particular kind of submission to a Lord who never cared— we could submit to a different kind of religion and, in it, find the blissful eternity we had been chasing all our lives. His words disarmed me, the look in his eyes compelling me forward. I ran my hands over his thighs and hauled them up, spreading them wide so he was curled up on the arch of his back, hole exposed for me. I positioned myself against the puckered muscle.

"Let me put the fear of God in you," I whispered.

Oliviero whimpered, and I pressed inside.

"*God!*" Oliviero moaned, hand fumbling up to catch my shoulder, the other thrusting out over the mensa to twist in the cloth. His face contorted, rapturous as he took me to the hilt. The pressure on my shoulder twisted to pain as Oliviero's nails dug in. I stroked his hips, assuring him, "You can take it. You're a good boy; I know you can take it."

His body shuddered, hand slipping into the tangle of my dark hair to pull me down. Our foreheads knocked together, both our skin slick with sweat. His hole flexed around my length, and so for many moments, I didn't move, though it was agonising waiting for him. When his hips relaxed—the tiniest, near imperceptible roll over my cock—I dragged myself out halfway and then clapped back, thunderous with my thrust.

Oliviero threw his head back with a cry, and as I thrust again and again in a slow, heavy pace, the chapel filled with a litany of moans echoing in the marble arches. We were watched by an audience of carved angels, by Jesus' stations of the cross, by God Himself: we were watched and not smote. Nothing could have pulled me away from the wet warmth of Oliviero.

Every gasp that emerged from him was shallow and airy. His eyes rolled to the back of his head. I splayed my hand over his chest, covered in a light down of blond-brown hair, curling over his tall and aroused pink nipples. I folded into him, tongue roaming over them, sucking at them, thrusting slow and controlled until he was so *wanting* Oliviero began to squirm impatiently, urging me for more.

I rocked back off him, hands gripping his pale ankles as if they were the reins of a horse tack, and I pulled his ass closer. Then, I drove forward with every bit of strength and desire I possessed in my body.

Oliviero howled, his loud cry petering out to a reedy whine as I thrust again and again into the warm pocket of his body. He was gulping air, crying out, *pathetic* and beautiful, as his cock bounced between us. Near translucent precum beaded at the tip, dribbling down the sides. It was complete submission; he gave me no resistance nor any help: he was rendered into nothing but a toy for my own desire, a receptacle for my cum. His eyes were heavy-lidded, as if every thrust forced his immortal soul further out of his flesh. I was defiling him. He could never return from this.

"What would they think if they knew?" I whispered, still thrusting hard. I had to shout it over the choral cry of his pleasure. "All the men who entrusted you with their faith? With all their worries and their doubts? What would they do if they knew you were a whore, just like Don Alessandro?"

Oliviero's whimper was shameful. His teeth slammed together in a desperate attempt to contain his cries. But then his eyes snapped open, and, through tears of shame, I saw his eyes roll back with sudden pleasure.

I didn't even have to touch him. All at once his cock bucked. His release shot into the air, splattering over my chest, and he clenched so firmly I couldn't have pulled free from him even if I'd wanted to. Oliviero's spent cock wobbled between us. Both his stomach and my chest were wet with our shared pleasure. I felt the urge building inside me—that moment where it all changed from *good* to *don't stop*. My body urged me to keep moving in him, but I took my time, dragging myself out so I felt every inch of his hole, every smooth moment, until the tight, puckered opening squeezed my sensitive glands. This rolling motion was an unbreakable rhythm. Not even God could have interfered in that moment. I buried myself all the way to the hilt and dragged out all the way to the tip, finding a perfect pace that let it all build, build, *build* until my core was tight and pulsing. Sweat drenched me,

"Oliv—"

I couldn't even form the word.

"*Yes!*" Oliviero whispered, astonishment curling in his tone.

With all the force of Hell, my body shuddered, and I came in him, the pleasure rolling in waves until the faintest aftershocks left me twitching inside him. He clenched again over my sensitive member—I had to pull free of him with a sharp, overstimulated hiss.

I collapsed against him, and he let me. Oliviero's hands spun through my hair, the sweat of my brow pressed to the sweat of his heaving chest.

We held each other for minutes until the heat of desire evaporated, and we were left chilly from our cooling sweat. And we cried.

They weren't tears of shame. They were great, heaving sobs of relief. Something had been taken from my back, a pressure I hadn't realised had been pressing down on me for a small eternity. Unburdened, I pressed my face into his neck and held him tightly.

"Thank you," I told him. "Thank you."

When I uncoupled from Oliviero and looked down at him, his eyes were staring off into the distance. His red-rimmed eyes could not see me.

I cupped his cheek and urged him to look at me. His head rolled limply.

"Do not do this to yourself," I told him. I could recognise shame clawing back into his body.

He flickered back into himself and blinked rapidly, brows crashing together in a weak frown. "What am I meant to do now?"

He sounded—accusatory. Upset. It was a misplaced anger, but I knew it well.

I leaned forward, and he let me kiss him, slow and languorous. When I pulled away, his cheeks were flushed again.

"You are beautiful," I told him. "And I have always wanted to do that to you. Maybe I should have, years ago; maybe I wouldn't have gone to such extremes to ease the suffering of my body if I had. But I will tell you this, Oliviero: do not be like me. Do not give yourself to an institution that won't repay you. It will take and take until you are a husk. You may still believe in God. You may still love Him—I will never fault you for your faith. But *people* corrupted His love for us. They made laws in His name. You do not have to follow them."

"How can you say such a thing when you have seen Hell?" he whispered, voice tiny.

"All I have experienced in Hell is my true self," I murmured. "All I have experienced is pleasure. I know myself better than I ever have."

He blinked at me, unconvinced, though with his body spent and latent pleasure throbbing behind his belly, I knew he would think on these words.

"Why did you come back?" he whispered. "Just for me? Have I failed a test from God?"

"It was no test for you. It was a test for me," He didn't know what to say to this. I kissed him again. "I feared what you thought of me. I know most of our brethren outside will doubt I was ever a good man."

He was still flushing as he looked at me. "You are a good man."

"Perhaps. But I am also a man who desires the pleasures of the flesh. In the eyes of the church, I cannot be a wholly good man."

"Then I..." his voice went high. I shushed him.

I pulled away from Oliviero. With the lack of contact, exposed as he was on the altar, he bolted upright and off. His body shook. The shame was eating him alive.

I pulled him into an embrace and waited for the shaking to stop.

"You can be absolved because God loves you. But so too can you enjoy your body and worship God if you so wish."

"Then why haven't you done so?" he sounded desperate. He clung to me, burying his beautiful face against my shoulder. "Stay. Stay here with me. Or we can leave—together. Let us go and find a place where we can worship God and share love with one another."

And I tell you, I was tempted. I imagined worshipping and loving Oliviero unabashed.

But I knew it wouldn't work. Not for me, not for someone who had worked to rid himself of the institution's foul grasp. Not when I imagined a life with Vassago and knew there would be no true freedom in a world that despised my love.

I looked Oliviero in the eye and told him, "Because God never answered my call. Only Asmodeus did."

I knew this was where our paths would divulge. Oliviero would never follow me into Hell; nor did I want him to. It was my path, and he was part of that path as I was on his.

"What will you tell them?" I asked.

He looked towards the door, frowning hard. "I do not know." Then, a visible swallow. "Not the truth. Only God will know the truth."

I nodded; it was for the best this way.

I turned to go, and he reached out for my hand. I paused, looking back at him.

"I don't know what I've done," he said, and for a long moment, I didn't expect him to say anything more. Then, quietly, he whispered, "But I thank you for it."

I slipped my hand free, turning it to plant a gentle kiss on the back of his hand.

"You deserve pleasure without shame," I told him, told myself.

And I left the abbey behind for good.

When I exited the double doors of the abbey, I walked right back into Dantalion's realm. The hellish bibliotheca, with its amber scent and dust mites and distant smog of sulphur, greeted me with a warmth that felt like a homecoming.

The demon sat in its wingback chair in the corner; its hands steepled over its knees. The bloody remains of the sigil lay at its feet. I had materialised before it and looked up at Dantalion, who stared at me with great interest.

"Well," it said, voice a low purr.

I swallowed, flushing. "Did that please you?"

"It most certainly pleased *you*."

I couldn't help but smile at that. I had wanted Oliviero for so long. To have given him pleasure, to have helped him on his own path, was a great thing for me to have done. And so, too, was the taking of my own pleasure. I had known what I wanted, and I had done it. I had told him I loved him. Love and pleasure and rough sex and blasphemy—all of it could co-exist.

Dantalion rose, its tall form towering in the corner of its

library. Carefully, it crossed around its sigil to me, arms outstretched. I did not know what to do with this sudden display of almost-affection. I let it lay its clawed hands upon my shoulders.

"Look up at me," it demanded, and so I looked.

Its many shifting faces oscillated between human and demon, male, female, other, until suddenly I was staring at the visage of Asmodeus itself, in the form of the first demon I had summoned all that time ago.

My entire heart seized.

The voice that came no longer belonged to Dantalion. It was the voice I had been hearing for my entire journey through Hell. I had crossed a lake of sin to reach this moment.

"You have done it," Asmodeus said. Gone was the violent, rough tinge to its voice, the anger at my insolence.

"You have been *such* a good little lamb for me, haven't you, Alessandro? My once-priest. My eternal whore."

I looked up into its eyes. "Dantalion. . .is pleased?"

"It called for my attention the moment you pushed that little priest down onto his own altar. The pair of us watched you defile his innocence in a house of God. We watched you love him, and he love you. How could we not be pleased?"

I flushed with pride and embarrassment and lust so deep it pulled at my very essence.

I wanted—I wanted Asmodeus. I wanted everything that came with servicing a demon. I wanted the immortality of my pleasure, to shuck my human past entirely. To forsake God most ardently, and for always.

To be Asmodeus'—forever.

"Come to me. Come to me now," Asmodeus cooed. Books flew from their place on the shelf, hurtling out to carve an arched doorway in the recess. Then a doorknob appeared, a snarled, angry silver thing, and the door was fully realised. A soft glow emanated from the cracks where it met the stone.

I felt a tug in my gut as if the anchor of my soul was caught on the sea floor. I knew that through those doors, Asmodeus waited.

It took its curled fingers and ghosted them over my cheeks. It leaned down and kissed me. Everything in me opened, a sluice gate of emotion and hope and desire. A certainty settled in me.

This was it.

And Asmodeus said, "Come and take your place as my immortal toy."

I walked to the door and opened it, and before me wound a staircase, up and up into red and black clouds.

A throbbing in my temples, in my heart, in my flesh. An incessant drumbeat urging me forward. It was the end of one journey, and the beginning of another.

Alessandro, transformed.

END

ABOUT THE AUTHOR

Lucien Burr has a background in Classics and is an author of dark fiction. His previous works include THE TERAS TRIALS and the PRINCE OF LUST series.

instagram.com/lucienburr

9 781763 864306